INCIDENT AT HORCADO CITY

**Center Point
Large Print**

**This Large Print Book carries the
Seal of Approval of N.A.V.H.**

INCIDENT AT HORCADO CITY

William Colt MacDonald

CENTER POINT PUBLISHING
THORNDIKE, MAINE

This Center Point Large Print edition
is published in the year 2008 by arrangement with
Golden West Literary Agency.

The text of this Large Print edition is unabridged. In other
aspects, this book may vary from the original edition.
Printed in the United States of America.
Set in 16-point Times New Roman type.

ISBN: 978-1-60285-277-8

Library of Congress Cataloging-in-Publication Data

MacDonald, William Colt, 1891-1968.
    Incident at Horcado City / William Colt MacDonald.--Center Point large print ed.
       p. cm.
    ISBN: 978-1-60285-277-8 (lib. bdg. : alk. paper)
    1. Large type books. I. Title.

PS3525.A2122I53 2008
813'.52--dc22

2008016673

I

Sheriff Beadle stood slouched in the roof overhang of the T.N. & A.S. railroad station, a wide-shouldered, rather gaunt-looking man in his late thirties, sombrero shoved back from a head of thinning hair. He wore a thick sandy mustache; his eyes were blue. Gray trousers were tucked into boottops at the knee; his flannel shirt was open at the throat. A worn cartridge belt sagged with the weight of the holstered six-shooter at his right thigh.

The usual loungers were beginning to gather to await the arrival of the eastbound T.N. & A.S. Limited. Most of them spoke to the sheriff, but he appeared scarcely to hear them. A woman, dressed for travel, emerged from the station, carrying a small grip. The lifting of the sheriff's hat was practically automatic when she spoke to him, and his eyes rested on her but a brief, polite moment.

The sheriff's deputy rounded the corner of the depot, drew to a halt and started twisting a Bull Durham cigarette. He said, "Mort, how do you figure Fletcher will take it?"

Sheriff Beadle drew a long sigh. "Scott Fletcher used to be right hot-headed—but it's over two years since I've seen him. Maybe he's changed. We'll just have to wait and see how the cards fall. Could be he'll behave sensible."

"Want I should wait and meet him with you?"

Mort Beadle considered, then shook his head. "I'll talk to him alone when he comes. You get back to Trail Street and keep your eyes open. Should you see him heading any place, looking like he's got blood in his eye, tag him close and don't let anything get started."

Even as he spoke a long-drawn whistle punctuated his remarks, and a humming sound rose from the rails beyond the platform. Somebody remarked, "Here she comes!"

Like some gigantic, prehistoric monster the engine flashed into view, shaking the very earth beneath the platform, and then, slowing, went thundering past the station to draw to a panting halt farther on. White steam drifted back to mingle with the swirling clouds of ebony black smoke. Brakes ground harshly. Cinders rained down.

Practically the first to step to the platform was a man of twenty-five, He was tall, wide-shouldered, good-featured, though at present his lips formed a thin straight line and his gray eyes were narrowed in suppressed anger. His blond beard had gone unshaven for days; his rumpled clothing looked as though he'd not undressed for many hours; his boots showed a lack of polish. Though he carried a small satchel in one hand, he had donned his belt and gun an hour before the train reached Horcado City.

The sheriff stepped forward to meet him, hand outstretched. He wasn't missing the Colt six-shooter showing beneath the other man's coat, though he

6

made no mention of it. "Scott, boy! You made right good time—" he started, then paused. "Scott, I can't put into words how I feel—I hated to be the one to telegraph you—I don't know what to say—your—your dad—I thought a heap—"

"Might as well save all that, Mort," Scott Fletcher said, tight-faced. "Words don't mean anything right now. Where is he?"

"Over to Flannery's Undertaking Parlors. I went ahead and made arrangements like I figured you'd want—well, Beriah Fletcher's going to be missed—I can't say how folks feel—"

He stopped. Scott Fletcher was already leaving the platform. The sheriff called to him, but the whistle of the departing train drowned the words. Beadle stood frowning, then strode to catch up with Fletcher. "You heading for the undertaker's, Scott?"

"Where else?" Scott Fletcher's words were cold, emotionless, but the sheriff sensed he was churning inwardly.

"Hadn't you best go to the hotel and clean up a mite, first?" the sheriff suggested. "There'll be services this afternoon at three."

Fletcher didn't reply. Beadle fell in at his side. "I'll go 'long with you." Fletcher didn't say anything. They walked along Deming Street and turned left on the principal thoroughfare of Horcado City, Trail Street, though often spoken of as Main. Two or three people spoke to Fletcher as he and the sheriff passed. If he heard them, he had no answer at the moment. They'd passed a livery, a saloon, a newspaper office, before Fletcher asked, "Do you happen to know if Mead Guthrie is in town?"

"Now, look here, Scott, don't jump to any wrong conclusions—"

"I'm not jumping. Who else would it be? He's hated Dad for years. He saw his chance and—"

"There's no proof of that. Now, you listen to me, son—"

"Just what happened?" Fletcher cut in.

"'That's what we don't rightly know. We found his body up at his place in Tourmaline. It could have laid there for days, except that he had a deal on with Webb Monroe. He and your father were to meet at the bank. Beriah didn't show up. Somebody went after him at the ranch. He wasn't there. So then a rider went up to Tourmaline. That's where they found him. I couldn't find one clue pointing to anybody, but I'm still working on it. The money ain't been found—"

"What money?" —sharply.

"The payment for the ranch. That was the deal with Monroe that was to be settled when your father didn't show up. But Monroe had already paid him the day before—"

"How much?"

"Fifty thousand."

Fletcher didn't reply as he stepped inside the building, Beadle drew a long uneasy sigh and started back the way he had come. He glanced across the street and saw his deputy had taken up a stance on the

8

opposite side of the street. The two men exchanged nods, and Beadle continued on his way. At the corner of Deming and Trail Streets he crossed diagonally and mounted the six steps leading to a gallery running along the front and one side of the hotel building. Two men sat in chairs there, booted feet on the railing.

One of them was Mead Guthrie, owner of the Bench-G outfit. He was a big man with bulky shoulders and grizzled gray hair, dressed in Levi's and woolen shirt, A wide sun-bleached mustache covered his thin lips. There was a 'hard something' about the man that always made the sheriff slightly uneasy.

The other man was Webb Monroe, of the Diamond-M Connected, and now claiming ownership, also, of the deceased Beriah Fletcher's Rafter-F Ranch. Monroe was a good-looking man also wearing cow-togs. He had dark hair and eyes and was probably thirty-five or thirty-eight. A smaller mustache adorned his upper lip, at present in need of trimming.

Monroe said, "I hear young Fletcher arrived." The sheriff nodded. Monroe continued, "How'd he take it?"

"How'd you expect he'd take it?" Beadle said curtly. He said abruptly to Mead Guthrie, "Look, Mead, why don't you get on your pony and go home for a spell?"

Guthrie cocked one narrowed eye at the sheriff. "Why in hell should I?" he asked harshly. "I come in to attend Fletcher's funeral. It's the least I can do, after all the years Fletcher and I didn't get along. When a man's dead, it's time for enmities to be dropped, I figure."

"Maybe they won't be dropped," the sheriff stated heavily. "Scott Fletcher hasn't changed a bit, as I see it. He looks to me like there's a volcano churning inside him. Me, I don't want any blow-ups around here. So I'd be obliged, Mead, if you'd clear out until I've had a better chance to talk to Scott. I might say the same to you, Webb. He thinks there's something wrong with your deal for the Rafter-F. I think myself—"

"Who me? Get out of town?" Webb Monroe acted astonished. "What could be wrong? I got Beriah Fletcher's bill-of-sale—"

"I'm just telling you two," Beadle cut in doggedly. "I don't want any trouble. No need you making it any harder for me—"

A belligerent snort was expelled from Mead Guthrie's lips. "I'm not riding out until I'm God damn good and ready to leave," he thundered. He patted the holster at his hip. "If Scott Fletcher figures I had ary thing to do with his old man's killing, all I ask is he come to me and ask questions. I won't take any lip from him, so he'd better ask real politelike—"

"Mead," Beadle pointed out in weary tones, "you must be expecting trouble. Otherwise, why the body-guard?"

Guthrie stared at the sheriff. "Bodyguard? What in hell you alludin' to, Mort?"

"Those two cowhands I saw you with a couple of hours back. They're strange to me—"

"So I hired two hands," Guthrie exploded. "I needed

10

two hands, Mort. Bodyguard my ass! I've yet to see the day when I needed any bodyguard. Hell! I never saw those two until I hired them. Ask Webb. He'll tell you—"

"All right, I take it back, Mead," Beadle said gloomily. A derisive snort exploded from Guthrie, his only notice of the apology. He settled more firmly in his chair, jerked his gun nearer to the front and sat glowering at the street.

Two men in cowtogs emerged from the front entrance of the hotel and made their way down the steps to the sidewalk. They crossed the road diagonally, unnoticed by the men on the porch, and moved into the entrance of the Flying Hooves Livery, which stood cater-cornered to the hotel.

At about the same moment, Scott Fletcher left the undertaker's establishment. The forty-five at his hip was slung low; his sombrero was jerked down on his forehead. His features were grim, ashen-white; grief had brought a look of insanity to his narrowed eyes. One mad thought dominated his whole existence: his father's death must be avenged, and the sooner the murderer was located, the better. If Mead Guthrie couldn't explain things to his satisfaction . . . and Webb Monroe too. . . .

He stepped determinedly to the roadway. Webb Monroe had risen to his feet. Mead Guthrie was sitting straighter in his chair.

A savage lance of white fire spurted from the shadowed livery entrance. A bullet kicked dust ten yards beyond Fletcher. Fletcher whirled, smoke and flame mushrooming from his gunbarrel in the direction of the livery entrance, the thundering explosion echoing along the street. From the shadows came a groan as a man went to his knees.

Something struck Fletcher's body and he stumbled and sprawled in the roadway. Another bullet kicked dust and gravel into his face. He struggled to his knees, bracing himself on one hand and released his second shot.

From the livery doorway came an anguished cry as the remaining ambushing cowhand staggered out to the walk, one hand clutching his stomach, the other his six-shooter as he strove to steady the gun for a final shot at Fletcher.

Fletcher fired a third time, the impact of the leaden slug whirling the cowhand half-around just as the man pulled trigger. The bullet flew wildly through space, stopping only when it had struck Deputy Stowe who was closing in at a run. Stowe paused in midstride, a look of amazement crossing his face. Then he, too, pitched to the earth.

II

Nearly four years later a rider drew to a puzzled halt midway through the Horcado Mountains. Gregory Quist, Special Investigator for the T.N. & A.S. Railroad, shoved back the flat-topped black sombrero from his thick tawny hair and mopped at his forehead with a bandanna. Noonday sun beat relentlessly down.

He wore corduroy trousers cuffed near the ankles of his riding boots, flannel shirt with a bandanna knotted at the throat. There was no cartridge belt, nor gun at his hip, though beneath his lightweight jacket he carried a Colt's .44 six-shooter in the shoulder holster. A small satchel was leashed to the back of his saddle.

Quist's topaz eyes again raised to the huge masses of rock barring his progress, then to the slopes on either side of the old stage road. "We're just plain stopped," he mused. "Could be, the road is clear again beyond this barrier. I'd best take a look."

He dropped reins over the pony's head, and stepped down from the saddle—something lithe, feline, in the easy movements—then paused to remove his coat and drop it across the pommel before ascending on foot the steep hillside slope at his right.

Then he looked east, beyond the rock barring the road, hoping to see an extension of the old stage trail. In this he was disappointed; there was nothing to see except a vast acreage of tumbled rock. There was no further sign of the trail he'd been following. He glanced around. To the south serrated peaks raised granite heads of grayish-pink color now bright in the sunlight. Off to his left, somewhat hazy in the distance, he thought he could see foothills and beyond that more level grass country. A mirage swam momentarily through the heat waves, depicting the buildings of a town, for the moment turned upside-down. The vision blurred, became elongated, distorted, wavered a few Moments and swiftly faded from view. "Could be that was Horcado City," he told himself. "I sure hope it's right side up by the time I get there."

He made his way back down the slope, swearing softly and impatiently when a bit of catclaw caught at his sleeve, and eventually reached the bottom. "Horse," he stated, "there's no way through this rock confronting us, so we've got some rough going ahead. But at least I have the right direction—I think."

A half hour later he again saw the rooves of what appeared to be a small settlement. He guided the buckskin down across a sort of swale, choked with brush, cactus and rock, and started to climb again. Abruptly, he checked the horse as something caught his attention in the shadow of a massive block of granite. At first sight it had appeared to be a large white ball, but Quist knew differently. His eyes narrowed as he dismounted and crossed the intervening yards to the shadow of the rock.

The thing that held the look of a white ball from a distance turned out to be the graying skull of what had once been a man. The skeleton was far from intact, the various bones being considerably scattered. Coyotes and buzzards had no doubt played their part in the skeleton's dismembering. Quist stooped down, the hollow, vacant eye sockets staring at him as though challenging him to reconstruct their final moments. Above the grinning teeth and slightly to one side, near what had once been a nose, was a small round opening in the skull.

Quist muttered, "That could have been made by a forty-five."

His gaze roved over the scattered bones. Several scraps of rotted, tattered clothing were scattered about. One shriveled and dry moccasin lay near, partly covered with coarse gritty sand. Quist uncovered its mate a moment later a few feet away. Then something else caught his eye. Half-buried in the loose earth was a bow. Quist drew it loose, the sand sifting from its six foot length. From either end hung, a few threads of tattered bowstring. No Indian string, this.

"And this bow is a mite finer than Injuns generally use, too," he stated, half-aloud. "Leastwise, it was at one time."

The bow had been weathered gray and had begun to show signs of checking. Quist. scraped a small section with one fingernail and found beneath the gray some sort of yellowish-orange wood. Both ends of the bow had been tipped with slotted pieces of cowhorn. One piece came loose in his hand while he was examining it. The other was also loose and showed a thin crack. The grip, or handle, was wound with rawhide strips and built up to fit a man's hand.

He moved in a stooped crouch around the bones, searching for arrows. There were none to be found. Neither did he find a quiver. And that seemed strange. Judging from the look of the bones they'd lain here a long time. Maybe someone else had taken the quiver. But in that case, why not the bow too? Quist made further search in the loose sand beneath the bones, straining the earth through his spread fingers. After a time he found an old forty-five bullet. Ten minutes of further searching uncovered some red glass beads and two more lead slugs. If there were more objects to be uncovered he didn't stay longer to learn. A glance at the sun showed him it was above the peaks to the west.

Leaving things as they were, except for the bow which Quist lashed to his saddle, he again mounted and continued his ride. The going became easier after a time, all downgrade now; the mesquite and cypress grew taller. Huge live oaks began to appear, their gnarled roots delving stubbornly into the stony earth. And then, abruptly, as he emerged from behind a tall craggy block of granite, Quist saw the buildings, the rooves of which he'd spied some time previously from a higher point in the mountains.

"Damned if it isn't a ghost town built up here," Quist muttered. "Wonder if there's anybody still living in those houses?"

There didn't appear to be. There was something eerie about the silence, broken only by the soft sound of the steady breeze through the mountains. Then Quist saw the sign, still hanging by a single rusted spike to a weathered post, the letters crudely formed and the paint blistered and faded: *Welcome to Tourmaline.*

"Prosperous-looking town," Quist chuckled as he guided the pony along the single street, cactus and sage dotting its length. The buildings were mostly shacks, built of odd bits of lumber; a few were of granite blocks. Windows were cracked or their panes missing altogether. Doors sagged open, hanging by one hinge.

Quist walked the buckskin the length of the silent street until he'd arrived at a sheer drop-off at the end. Then he turned back, frowning. He'd seen nobody, heard no man's voice, but every instant some sixth sense told him he was being watched, but by whom he'd no idea. It didn't bother him particularly, but he didn't like it either. Starting back he lifted his jacket from the pommel and put it on, his gaze intent now on the single building that had caught his interest, a wide blocky building constructed of granite and adobe. Its doors and windows were tightly shut, the panes of glass intact. It was situated in the middle of town, with its back against the sheer granite wall. The building had recently been whitewashed, which meant to Quist that someone still lived here.

As he drew abreast of the place, Quist slowed pace, half-inclined to dismount and knock at the door. But he could think of no good reason for doing so. And while he was considering the matter the door opened abruptly and a tall blond man stood frowning in the entrance.

"You looking for me, mister?" the man demanded, a certain belligerency showing in his tones.

Quist studied him a moment. The fellow wasn't wearing a gun. Nor did he hold one in either hand. Still, you could never tell how fast an angry man might produce a weapon.

"No, I wasn't," Quist said quietly. "Are folks supposed to be looking for you?"

The man flushed. "Not any more—I hope." He forced a laugh but there was little humor in it.

"Maybe you're lucky," Quist chuckled.

The blond man scowled. "Anything in particular you want in Tourmaline?"

"Nothing I can think of right now. You all alone here?"

"This is a ghost town, mister. There's nobody here but me." He added sarcastically, "Sorry the hotel isn't open."

"Look," Quist stopped him, "there's no need to get proddy with me. I somehow got off the trail coming through the mountains. I'm headed for Horcado City."

"You've got about five miles to go yet—five or six."

"I know. I could see the buildings from the end of your street. Nice view you have there."

"If you like that sort of view," the man said shortly.

"I do," Quist said cheerfully. "I like ghost towns too—especially when they're haunted."

The tall blond man's scowl deepened. "What do you mean—haunted?"

"Lady ghosts," Quist said in a mocking half-whisper. "You've already stated you're alone here, so it must have been a lady ghost that dropped her hankie near your door, and no man your size ever made such small boot-prints—"

The door abruptly slammed shut. Grinning widely, Quist started the pony again and moved along the street. Beyond the point where he had entered Tourmaline, Quist saw a high stack of bales of straw, attached to the front of which at about man's height, was a large square of canvas, upon which had been painted, in various colors, the concentric circles representing a target of some sort. It appeared to Quist to have been plentifully punctured. A tall live oak tree had shielded the target from Quist's eyes as he entered the town.

Quist eyed the target with some disgust. "No wonder that hombre didn't have a gun on him, if he needs a target that size to practice his shooting. He's just showing good sense in not toting a gun yet, I reckon, until he learns something about lead throwing."

III

Only a faint afterglow of light above the western peaks of the mountains remained by the time Quist guided the buckskin pony along the main thoroughfare of Horcado City.

Quist had already spied the sheriff's office on the southwest corner of Trail and Caddo, but he rode a block or so farther before turning back to dismount and drop his reins over the tierail. The roof of the fairly large building extended out to uprights built at the edge of the sidewalk. Between the uprights was a sign: *Office of Sheriff—Tasajillo County.* Two steps led to the porch fronting the building. There were two windows at the front and between was an open doorway. Light shone from within, thrown by an oil lamp suspended above the sheriff's roll-top desk. At the back a closed door led to the cells.

Quist crossed the porch and stepped within the office. Mort Beadle swung around in his swivel chair and said "Howdy. What can I do for you?"

"You the sheriff?"

"Right. Beadle's the name—Mort Beadle, Stranger here, aren't you?" Quist said he was and gave his name. The two shook hands and Quist pulled up a chair. Beadle said, "You on business here?"

Quist nodded. "I work for the Texas Northern and Arizona Southern road. Left Flaxton early this morning intending to cut through the mountains, but the trail reached a dead end and slowed me up."

"Too bad. Somebody must have told you to take the old stage road." Quist nodded again. Beadle continued, "Sho', that road ain't been open for nigh three years now. Don't know what happened, but there must have been a quake over in them mountains or a landslide. Anyway about half a mountain just reared up one time and spilled itself down to fill up that road. Stage company had to locate another pass. It comes down from further north now. Somebody just misdirected you, I reckon."

"That's the case. One of these days there'll be a train coming down through those mountains—T.N. & A.S., I hope."

"Don't doubt it, the way this country is building up.

Look at the way Horcado City has boomed. We even got our own brickyard and lumber-mill now. And there's a school and two churches gone up the past two years, out on east Atacosa Street—" He paused and sheepishly brushed back his sandy mustache with one hand. "But you didn't come here to listen to civic boastings. What's on your mind?"

"When I was coming through the mountains this afternoon I ran across a skeleton. Thought it should be reported."

The sheriff straightened in his chair. "Skeleton?" He scowled. "Don't know of anybody's been missing hereabouts. Haven't had any trouble for a long spell now. But, a skeleton, you say. That means he died some spell back—"

"The bones had been more or less scattered around. Animals and buzzards responsible, I suppose. Such bits of clothing as I saw were just rags. The man had been shot as I see it."

"T'hell you say. And nothing to show who he was, eh?"

"Looked like an Indian to me from the shape of the skull and so on. A few patches of hair clung to the skull; looked like Indian hair. There was an old bow half-buried in the sand. I—"

"Oh, Injun, eh?" Beadle relaxed. "Nothing to worry over, Mr. Quist. Every so often somebody reports Injun skeletons found over in those hills. We had a bunch of Tonkawas around here years ago. They used to live up in the Horcado Mountains. They'd been run out by the

21

Comanches. The Tonkawas finally joined with the whites to lick the Comanches, but even that got too tough for some of them. They drifted down to this country and then gradually vanished—I don't know where to. A mean miserable bunch, most of 'em. They had a rep for cannibalism, so maybe it wasn't coyotes that disturbed those bones, Like's not a bunch of the skeleton's friends jumped him. 'Course I can ride up there and make an investigation, if you say so."

"I don't say so. It's up to you. You're the sheriff of this county."

Beadle frowned. "Could you tell me just about where you found the skeleton?"

Quist considered. "I could lead you up there, but as to describing the exact place—"

"Not by any means. I couldn't think of asking you to lead me there, Mr. Quist. Sho', now, you've got your own business to 'tend to. I reckon we'd just better forget the whole business, unless something else comes up. Like I say, them Tonkawas was more or less miserable specimens of humanity. I never knew but one of 'em to amount to much—"

He broke off as a man of thirty-three or -four, wearing a deputy's badge, entered the office. "I'm going to eat my supper now if it's all right with you, Mort—" he started, then paused as Beadle introduced him:

"This is Mr. Quist, Jeff. My deputy, Jeff Crawford." Quist shook hands with the deputy. Beadle continued, "Mr. Quist works for the railroad, Jeff."

22

Jeff Crawford was a stocky man of medium height, with brown hair and eyes. He looked very capable and the gun and holster at the right hip were well-worn as though they had seen a lot of use. He was dressed in denim shirt, an open vest and bibless overalls; his boots had been brushed that. day though his sombrero showed signs of long wear and was slightly battered.

He drew out Durham tobacco and papers and passed them to Quist. The two men rolled smokes, Crawford leaning against the door jamb. He said, when the cigarettes were lit, "T.N. & A.S., eh? What sort of work do you do, Mr. Quist? You look like cowfolks to me."

Quist laughed. "I've worked cows in my time. Now—we-ell—you might say I'm a sort of line-rider for the company."

"Figured it was something like that," Beadle said. "Sort of ride around checking on rails and seeing that no telegraph wires are down and so on, I suppose." Before Quist had time to reply, Beadle turned to the deputy. "Coming through the Horcados this afternoon, Jeff, Mr. Quist found the skeleton of a redskin and felt obliged to report it. Another of those Tonkawas, I reckon."

"Could be," Crawford nodded. "You're not the first man to find bones up in those rocks. Want I should investigate, Mort?"

The sheriff shrugged. "I don't know any particular reason you should."

"You're sure it was an Indian?" the deputy asked.

"Not sure, no," Quist replied, "but it looked that way to me. There was an old bow there, a pair of moccasins. I sifted the sand some and located some lead chunks and a few glass beads. The skull was shaped like an Indian's. I've seen a good many from time to time so I don't think I'm wrong."

"I guess we can forget it, Jeff," from Beadle. "Some of his pals jumped him, maybe ate him for all we know. It's nothing to fret about—"

"How come you sifted the sand?" Crawford asked. "What did you expect to find?"

Quist shrugged and gave a short laugh. "Didn't expect anything. I just happen to be curious that way. Something else has aroused my curiosity too. What about that ghost town up there?"

"Tourmaline?" from Crawford. "You came that way, eh? See anybody around up there?"

"One man. Tall blond fellow. He wasn't too cordial."

"That'd be Scott Fletcher," the sheriff said heavily. "He had some trouble here a few years back. Since then he keeps to himself mostly. Makes bows and arrows. Sells 'em—I don't know where. Oh, he's law-abiding now and all that. It's just that he don't mix with folks. Could be he's gone sour on life. Don't know's I'd blame him either."

"I suppose there's some business in bows and arrows. Tourists buy 'em for their kids to play Indian with," Quist commented. "But why a ghost town up there? Was there ever any mining hereabouts?"

"There was some tourmaline found up there," Beadle explained. Tourmaline is a mineral, Mr. Quist, in case you don't know. It's found in greens and pinks. Sometimes both colors show in one chunk. It's used in making jewelry. Anyway, word got around that a gem mineral had been found in the Horcados, and the stampede was on. Gem mineral spelled diamonds to most folks. So that's how Tourmaline came to be settled. It didn't last long."

"Say, Mr. Quist," Jeff Crawford said suddenly, "your name doesn't happen to be Gregory, does it?" Quist nodded. The deputy shot a quick glance at Beadle, but nothing registered. "Cripes Almighty, Mort, don't you know who this is? Mort, this is the famous T.N. & A.S. detective. We've read about you, Mr. Quist—"

Quist shrugged it off. "Railroad dick, trouble-shooter—jeepers! it's nothing to get excited about. Well, my stomach is beginning to feel like my throat was cut. I'll push on and get some supper—"

He rode first to the livery stable and gave instructions for the care of the horse. Then, unlashing the bow and his satchel, he left the livery and headed diagonally across to the Inwood Hotel which stood on the corner. Mounting the steps to the gallery, he passed the front entrance and went in the hotel bar doorway at the side. There was no one in the bar at the moment, except the bartender who sat on a stool at one end. He was a pot-bellied individual with slicked-down hair and a yellow diamond in his neck-tie. The apron tied about his waist was clean and he wore sleeve garters on the arms of his white shirt. He was known as Keg Hooper. He slid from his stool as Quist entered.

Quist gave his order. "Beer—and I don't want it iced."

"You're the one who's paying for it, mister," the barkeep smiled. He set out a bottle, opened it and shoved a shining glass on the bar. Quist ignored the glass, raised the bottle to his lips and set it down only when it had been emptied. Then he drew a long sigh of satisfaction.

"I've been waiting for that ever since noontime," he stated.

"You act like you'd crossed a broiling desert to get here." Hooper eyed him curiously.

Lugging the bow, a package of beer bottles and the satchel, Quist passed through a door leading to the lobby, empty at the moment save for an elderly clerk with gray sideburns behind the desk counter. He glanced curiously at the bow Quist carried, but made no comment while Quist registered and asked for a corner room with a cross draft "if possible."

He pulled down the window shades and looked about. It was the usual hotel room. There was a window in the front wall, overlooking Trail Street and another in the side wall on the Deming Street side. Double bed, dresser, commode holding a pitcher of water and wash bowl, and a small table to hold the lamp. A straight-backed chair and a rocker were included. The carpet with some sort of figured pattern was worn. The room was clean; that was the main thought in Quist's mind.

He opened a bottle of beer, peeled off his shirt and got from the satchel his shaving things. By the time he'd donned a fresh shirt and bandanna the bottle was finished. His mind kept returning to the skeleton he'd found and the bow.

He shrugged his shoulders impatiently. "I'd best forget it and go down for some supper before the dining room closes." He got into his coat, used the soiled bandanna to brush dust from his flat-topped black sombrero and turned down the lamp. Just as he started for the door, key in hand, he heard footsteps in the hall. Then came a knock. Quist opened the door so suddenly his visitor jerked back in surprise, and couldn't find his tongue for a moment.

Quist said, "You want to see me?"

"Er—er—yes. Won't keep you a minute. Your name's Quist, ain't it?" Quist nodded. The other went on, "My name's Daulton." From the man's clothing, Quist judged him to be a cowhand. He was spare, of medium height, with somewhat shifty eyes that refused to look squarely at Quist.

"What can I do for you, Daulton?"

"Well—er—it's like this. The old goat downstairs—"

"You mean the hotel clerk?"

"That's it. Well, it's like this. He said you were carrying an Injun bow when you come here and—well — I think it belongs to me—"

27

"What gives you that idea?"

"You found it, didn't you?"

"Who told you that?"

"We-ell, I just sort of heard it around someplace. I guess it was the old goat, mebbe. You see, it belonged to my kid. He likes to play Injun and he lost it and I figured—"

"Where'd he lose it?"

"Well, I couldn't say exact. Out beyond town some-place, I reckon. Come to think of it, I think he said down by the creek—"

"I didn't find it near any creek, so it can't be your bow, or your kid's."

"Could be he was mistaken, Mr. Quist. Look, it's like this, I'd hate to see the little tyke disappointed. Suppose I just give you a couple of bucks and we'll let the kid think he's got his bow back—"

"The bow's not for sale." Quist shook his head.

"I'll make it five," —eagerly.

"Without even seeing if it's worth five bucks."

"I'll take a chance on that, Quist."

Quist studied the man, not liking his looks. "You're quite a gambler, aren't you? But I'm afraid five isn't enough. You'll have to raise the ante."

"All right, I understand. Ten dollars says I get that bow."

"Ten dollars," Quist said sharply, "is a liar. And you are too. Now, clear out."

And before Daulton had an opportunity to reply, Quist closed the door in his face. He heard some muttered curses beyond the door, then the receding footsteps as Daulton departed.

Quist went to the table, got a bottle of beer and opened it, his forehead furrowed with thought. "Looks like that might be a mighty expensive bow I found," he muttered. "Now why is somebody so anxious to get hold of it? And who put Daulton on the trail? Let me see, who did I tell about it? Sheriff Beadle. His deputy. The bartender mentioned it. Daulton said the clerk told him—oh, hell! I'm into something and I might as well stay with it."

He put down the bottle, turned up the lamp-wick and jerking out a drawer of the small table found some writing paper, pen and ink. Seating himself he penned a note to Jay Fletcher:

> *. . . and now I'm here in Horcado City. There's something stirring I don't like. Are you related to Scott Fletcher who lives near here? He's been into trouble of some sort, and I'd like to learn what it is, and if it could concern the company in any way. So I'll be staying on unless you have something more pressing for me to do. Yrs, etc. Greg.*

Quist smiled as he folded the letter and inserted it in an envelope, then addressed it to the T.N. & A.S. Superintendent of Divisions at El Paso, who, coincidentally, happened also to be named Fletcher.

He again turned down the lamp, and left his room, locking the door behind him.

IV

Quist made his way thoughtfully down the stairs to the lobby and stopped at the desk. "Hope everything is satisfactory, Mr. Quist," the aged clerk said.

"Just fine," Quist nodded. "A man named Daulton came up to my room a few minutes ago. Know anything about him?"

"Very little. He's in town frequently. He's not the type I'd have anything to do with."

"I can understand that. What does he do?"

"I'm not sure, but I do know he worked for Mr. Webb Monroe on the ranch. He's a cowpuncher, I believe. What? No, I've never heard he had any family, let alone a small son."

"So you probably didn't tell him I arrived here with an 'Injun bow' in my hand as he claimed."

"I certainly did not," the clerk stated indignantly. "Naturally I noted it when you arrived, but what baggage guests carry is none of my concern. Daulton entered, asked for your room number and started upstairs before I could stop him. For all I knew he had an appointment with you. I'm sorry if anything has gone wrong—"

"It hasn't. Don't worry. My curiosity was aroused, that's all."

"I'm glad you've not been troubled. Mr. Quist, if you plan on dining with us, the restaurant closes in a half hour."

"I'd best hurry then. Thanks."

Quist passed through the doorway at the right of the stairway, through a sort of sitting room and into the restaurant at his left, which occupied the rear of the hotel with one wall flanking the outside gallery on Deming Street. There weren't more than a dozen tables in the dining room, and only three of these were occupied. A family party of six sat near one wall. A man and woman were seated at a center table. In the front corner a man sat alone, though a woman stood talking to him in low tones. Quist made his way to a far corner, next to a window, hung his hat on a hook and sat down. The man talking to the woman said something and gestured toward Quist. The woman turned quickly and then approached.

"Good evening, Mr. Quist," she said as she approached. "It is Mr. Quist, isn't it?" Her voice was a liquid contralto.

"Right." Quist got to his feet and liked the firm handshake the woman offered. "You people catch on fast in this town. But I wonder how you knew."

"That's part of my business, here, to know guests. I manage this dining room for Mr. Inwood. Please sit down. I could tell you I got your name from the register, and that would be true. On the other hand, I think by this time it must be all over town that the famous railroad detective, Gregory Quist, is paying us a visit. Oh, yes, I'm Mrs. Monroe. There'll be a waitress here in a minute for your order. Up to a few minutes ago we've been rushed and the girls are overworked—" At

31

that moment a Mexican girl in a white apron approached the table. "Take good care of Mr. Quist, Estrella. Enjoy your dinner, Mr. Quist."

Mrs. Monroe nodded, turned and left the dining room, followed by Quist's admiring glance. The waitress' voice brought him back to earth: "Meester Queest, you are giving thee ordair . .?"

"Oh, sorry, I was thinking of the dessert," Quist said absentmindedly. The girl told him what there was left to order and Quist asked for roast beef and the "fixings."

Halfway through his meal, the waitress brought a bottle of beer with the statement, "Weeth the complimen' of thee hotel, *señor.*"

He had finished his dessert and was drinking a second cup of coffee when the man at the far table who'd been talking to Mrs. Monroe when Quist entered the dining room, rose and sauntered down the room. He was smiling as he reached Quist's table.

"Allow me to introduce myself, Mr. Quist. I'm Webb Monroe. I run the Diamond-M Connected. Heard so much about you, here and there, that I didn't want to miss the opportunity of welcoming you to Horcado City. Of course, it's all over town you've arrived here, so I had no trouble guessing—"

"Mrs. Monroe is your wife, then?" Quist asked.

"Ex-wife," Monroe said casually. "Leila didn't care for ranch life. She preferred the town. In a way I couldn't blame her. It's rather dull for a beautiful woman out there—and I think you'll admit, Mr. Quist, she is a beautiful woman, if I do say it myself. We're perfectly good friends, as you can realize. Oh, have a cigar?" —passing one across the table.

Quist refused with thanks and drew out his Durham and papers. Monroe continued, "Expect to be here long, Mr. Quist?"

Quist shrugged and lighted his cigarette. "That's hard to say. Company business, you understand."

"Oh, sure. Naturally I couldn't expect you to tell me about it." For some reason he appeared relieved, Quist noticed. After a moment he rose from the table. "Well, I'll be glad to help you get acquainted around here, if there's anybody you particularly want to meet."

Quist tried a shot in the dark: "I've already made the acquaintance of a few—your sheriff and deputy, a man in Tourmaline—a bartender who sells good beer—one or two others—"

"Fletcher?" Color rose in Monroe's face and a momentary scowl crossed his features. "Scott Fletcher. I'm sorry Fletcher and I don't see eye to eye. He has some mistaken idea about me that I've never been able to clear up. I'd rather not talk about it. You understand, I hope."

"Of course," Quist replied. Monroe gave him a short nod, turned and left the dining room, some of the jauntiness having departed from his bearing. Quist gazed thoughtfully after the man. "I've a hunch I hit a raw nerve. I've got Monroe bothered. *Hmmm.*"

Quist left some money on his table, extinguished his cigarette, got his sombrero and left the dining room. Mrs. Monroe met him at the doorway.

"I hope you enjoyed your supper, Mr. Quist."

"The food was excellent, Mrs. Monroe—"

She smiled, dimples showing in her cheeks. "Then we'll be able to expect you back?"

He laughed. "I think it's going to be pretty hard to keep me away."

The color rose in her cheeks. Quist doffed his hat and passed through the lobby and out to the street. Leila Monroe gazed after him. "So that's the great railroad detective they say has a way with women. Well"—a frown creased her forehead—"it's possible they're right."

There weren't many people abroad by the time Quist stepped out on the hotel gallery. He stood in the shadow to one side of the entrance and gazed both ways along the street. A general store, just across the roadway was closed and dark, but in its recessed doorway Quist could plainly make out a man's form. One of the clerks, perhaps, who had just locked the door and was waiting for someone.

Quist strode casually down the steps from the gallery and turned right, crossing Deming Street, past the bank and a ladies' wear shop. A real estate office with a dim light burning at the rear furnished an excuse to pause and look into the window. As Quist turned, he caught a quick glimpse of the man who'd been standing in the general store doorway. The fellow had emerged into the open and crossed the street, and for a moment the lights from the hotel fell across his face. Quist recognized the man then. It was

Daulton, the fellow who had tried to buy the bow. And Daulton was a Webb Monroe employee.

"Things are beginning to look interesting," Quist laughed softly, continuing on his way. "So now somebody's put a tail on me. But I'm damned if I can figure out why. What in the devil is going on? And what am I suspected of doing? Somebody must be getting nervous."

He walked on, crossed Crockett Street, then crossed over and started back, passing a frame building that called itself the Stockmen's Hotel, a fleabag. He swerved suddenly and saw his 'tail' duck into a doorway. Quist chuckled and kept going. Reaching the Flying Hooves Livery, he entered and talked to the man on duty for a few minutes, ascertaining that his horse had been well cared for. At the rear of the livery, past the double row of stalls and vehicles, a wide doorway stood open. Instead of returning to Trail Street, Quist departed by the rear. Reaching the open once more, he gazed about. Several yards beyond, the T.N. & A.S. rails glistened beneath the starlight. To his left, the distance of a half-block, he spied the railroad station. Lights shone dimly from its windows; the freight house at the farther end was dark.

There was no one on the platform when he reached the depot, nor was anyone waiting within when he opened the door. He crossed the room and glanced through a window. Daulton was moving stealthily through the shadows. The man glanced up and saw Quist watching him. Thereupon he abandoned his

35

attempt at stealth, and came boldly on. Quist chuckled. "Daulton is a better tail than I figured. Probably wants to learn what I'm doing here."

He went to the grilled window in the partition, beyond which he could hear the *clackety-clack-clack* of the telegraph instrument. The stationmaster, a middle-aged man named Lane Johnson, approached to ascertain his wants. "Ticket, sir?"

Quist shook his head and produced credentials to prove his identity, then gave Johnson the letter he'd written to Jay Fletcher. "When westbound Number Seventeen comes through, give this envelope to the conductor. Tell him I want it rushed through to Mr. Fletcher. In this way we'll save time that might be lost at the post office."

"I'll take care of it, Mr. Quist. Anything else I can do for you?"

"I had some business up at Flaxton, and while I was there I had a telegram from Fletcher telling me to come here and get the details on that freight robbery you reported last week."

Johnson laughed. "Too bad you had to make a long trip for nothing. That freight robbery didn't amount to much. We had a car on a siding waiting to be filled before sending it on. It was broken into and two cases of whisky were stolen. There was little else in the car worth stealing at the time. Anyway, Deputy Jeff Crawford ran down the culprits a couple of days ago. They were just a couple of no-goods in town who never have any money and are always cadging drinks. So when they suddenly showed up drunk all the time, Jeff Crawford got suspicious. He put a little pressure on them and they confessed. They're in jail now, awaiting trial. I already wired to El Paso about that. Maybe Fletcher didn't get the news yet, it was so unimportant."

"Could be. Glad it wasn't more serious. Thanks for taking care of things."

"You're welcome. Shame you had to come here just for that I suppose you'll be leaving tomorrow."

Quist shrugged. "I may hang around a few days. Nice town. I need a rest. Good night." The station man said good night.

Quist stepped outside, closing the door after him. Sitting on a bench outside the station was Daulton. Quist said pleasantly, "Good evening, Mr. Daulton. Waiting for a carload of bows to arrive?"

"You think that's funny, Quist?" Daulton said sullenly.

"Maybe not, if you feel that way. All right, I'll say something that's not funny. If you don't quit following me around I'm going to knock your head out from under your hat. No, wait, don't deny it. You followed me from the hotel west on Trail Street, and when I returned on the other side, you were right behind me. And now you're here. What's the answer?"

Daulton's eyes slid sidewise. "Hell, can't a man take a walk if he likes?"

"Not too close behind me, he can't. I don't like it. And now you're down here at the station, I suppose, just because you like to watch the choo-choo go past."

"That's nearer to fact than you might think," Daulton bridled. "I was just tryin' to make up my mind if I should go visit my old mother in Las Cruces, only I ain't got the price of a ticket—"

"And yet you had ten bucks to offer for an old bow. Come again, Daulton, and think fast." Daulton didn't say anything. He looked up at Quist and then away. Quist said, "I tell you what you do. Go into the station and tell Johnson I said you were to have a ticket to Las Cruces and charge it to me. It'll work to a benefit for two people. First your dear old mother will get a look at your ugly mug again, and I won't have to look at it any more. What do you say?"

"You act like you're lookin' for trouble, Quist."

"Sure, I am," Quist replied. "Would you like to help me look for it? Just get up on your feet. No? Then be sure you stay on that bench. If you get up before I'm out of sight, you can bet your sit-spot your old mother won't see her wayward boy again." He reached down suddenly, jerked the gun from Daulton's holster and hurled it far across the tracks and into the brush on the far side. "I just didn't like to take a chance on turning my back to you. And remember what I said about leaving that bench. Good night, Daulton."

Daulton didn't reply, but only huddled a little lower on the bench. He didn't even raise his head to look at Quist. Quist delayed a moment longer, then made his way down from the station platform, turned into Deming Street and headed for the hotel.

"Maybe I treated Daulton a mite rough," he speculated, "but if trouble is due to break I might as well let people know just where I stand. Anyway, Daulton can now hurry back to whoever put him to tailing me and tell that he heard me talking about Fletcher—though I doubt he'll guess it wasn't Scott Fletcher I was talking about. Could be I can scare somebody into making a wrong move—but why, I still can't figure out."

V

Over a breakfast of pancakes and ham the following morning, Quist found but small opportunity to talk to Leila Monroe. She gave him a quick pleasant nod when he was seated and sent one of the two waitresses to see to his order. The dining room was filling fast, mostly, Quist judged, with town merchants. He drained his coffee cup, twisted a cigarette and left the dining room, almost bumping into Webb Monroe who was just entering. The two men stopped a moment to exchange conversation. Quist said,

"You must have stayed in town overnight."

Monroe nodded. "It got later than I thought, so I got a room at the hotel here. Leila isn't the only one who prefers being in town to the ranch. I've got a good foreman, so things go along out there just as well as if I was on the job. This is lucky meeting you. I wanted to see you a minute."

"What about?"

"Look, I'm never awake mornings until I've had

some coffee. Could I meet you out on the gallery in a half hour or so?"

Quist nodded. "Judging from the crowd in the dining room it may take you longer than a half hour. But I'll be there."

Keg Hooper stood behind his bar commiserating with a doleful-looking individual in town's-clothing who looked as though he had a hangover and was getting some 'of the hair of the dog that bit him.'

"And you take my advice," Keg was saying, "and you'll find beer will do you more good. Or just plain bitters—" He broke off as Quist entered and moved down the bar. "Ah, another early bird. The top of the morning to you, Mr. Quist."

"And it's not a worm I came in for," Quist laughed.

The barkeep placed beer and a glass on the counter. Quist poured a glassful. The hangover individual at the far end looked resentfully at the two. "Gawd, it's noisy in here," he complained. "So early in the day, too." He finished his drink and walked slowly out of the bar.

"There's nobody like a barkeep for hearing all the news and knowing the country. What's the layout hereabouts? What cow outfits are important?"

Hooper tugged at the lobe of one ear as though marshaling his thoughts. "Well, to begin with there's the Horcado Mountains running down from the north. They split to the shape of an upside-down Y. The branch to the east is known as the Little Horcados. Then there's Horcado Creek which heads up in the northwestern mountains and flows down through our valley between the two branches of the upside-down Y." With a wet finger he traced a map on the bar. "Now you see, Horcado Creek splits about the middle of the valley. One fork runs due south, and the other fork heads east and south. It sort of peters out at the end and sinks into a stretch of flats just before it reaches the foothills of the Little Horcado Mountains, Clear?"

"I'm still with you."

"Mead Guthrie is the biggest owner here. His Bench-G covers a good section of land above Horcado Creek and most of the land below the place where the creek forks south. He's to the west. Across the south fork lies Webb Monroe's spread, the Diamond-M Connected. It's just a diamond design with two legs running down from the side points of the diamond, the lower v of the diamond forming part of the M. Then to the southeast of the Diamond-M lies the Slash-O, run by Otto Wagner. And south and farther east of Wagner's place is Cody Hayden's Rocking-H. The buildings of none of them are more than twenty miles or so away. Then, of course, there's three or four little outfits scattered around that can't make up their minds if they want to run cows or push a plow."

"This Guthrie—what sort of a hombre is he?"

Keg Hooper shrugged. "I don't figure he's too well-liked. Got a habit of riding rough shod over folks. He's a big grizzly bear of a man. Webb Monroe is all right, I guess. Most folks seem to like him. He's full of hell at times and carries a sort of wild crew that Jeff Crawford has trouble controlling come paydays. But Sheriff Beadle is right rough on that sort of thing. Otto Wagner's a good-natured Dutchy—most of the time—though I've seen him show a spell of temper on occasion. Cody Hayden's a good hombre. Nice-looking cuss. Rather fancies himself a ladies' man, I figure."

"Speaking of ladies, we now come to Leila Monroe. What's the set-up in that direction."

Hooper's eyes twinkled. "She got to you too, eh? Howsomever, you know the old saying, 'No gentleman discusses a lady in a barroom.' "

"Let's pretend we're not gentlemen for a spell, Keg. I'm curious about her, to tell the truth."

Hooper laughed. "You and how many other gents around here? Ever since she left Webb and went to Dallas for her divorce and then came back here, the boys been buzzing around her like bees around a hive. No, I don't know why she returned here. She and Webb seem friendly when they run into each other. It seemed sort of queer at first, but now nobody gives it a thought. She tried running a bonnet shop for women when she first come back, then she sold that and has been running the dining room for Mr. Inwood ever since. Between you and me, I think Inwood would like to marry her."

"Inwood 'and how many other gents around here?' " Quist repeated Hooper's words.

"Ain't it the truth!"

"Now," Quist prodded, "just what do you know about a man named Scott Fletcher?" Hooper frowned and Quist took a sip of beer before saying, "The sheriff mentioned that Fletcher had some trouble around here."

"Hell, that's nearly four years ago," Hooper stated indignantly. "Aren't folks ever going to forget it? Scott had enough hard luck as it was. Sure, I remember when he was full of oats and vinegar and used to raise a lot of hell around town, but he was away when it happened and even if he did have a rep as a fast man with a gun, if what he thought was true—oh, hell, maybe you're not interested."

"What do you think I came in here for?"

"Beer, naturally. All right, there's the story as I know it, but I may be shy on details. All the Bench-G holdings south of Horcado Creek and west of the south fork of the creek was once Rafter-F property, owned by Beriah Fletcher, Scott's father. Beriah Fletcher and Guthrie had some trouble one time and they never did get along. Guthrie tried to buy him out to get rid of him. Fletcher wouldn't sell. Then, about four years back, when Scott was out on the west coast someplace, Webb Monroe came to town one day and announced that he had bought the Rafter-F. Nobody could believe it at first, until Monroe showed a bill-of-sale with Fletcher's signature on it, and said that he was to meet Fletcher at the bank to sign papers all regular. But Fletcher didn't show up. Eventually, his dead body was found up at Tourmaline. He'd been killed with .45s and an arrow—"

"An arrow?"

"There was an arrow stuck in his back, clean to the heart. That made it look like Indian work. Sheriff Beadle sent word for Scott to come home. Scott arrived with blood in his eye, convinced that something crooked was going on, aside from his father's murder. He stated that Monroe never had that much money—the price for the ranch was fifty thousand—and to top that he brought up the fact that his father and Guthrie had always been enemies. So after going to the undertaker's, he started out to find both Guthrie and Monroe. He told the sheriff he just intended to question them, but he was wearing his gun, so nobody knows what he had in mind."

"An angry man with a gun? There's not much doubt what he had in mind, is there?"

"It's not for me to say. He saw Guthrie and Monroe seated on the hotel gallery out there and started for 'em. Just as he was passing the livery stable firing broke out. Who started it, depends on which witnesses you believe. There are those who say that Scott was already reaching for his gun. Others say the two cowpunchers hidden in the shadow of the livery door opened fire first on Scott. Scott managed to plug both men, but got hit himself, not too seriously. The sheriff's deputy at the time, a nice fellow named Stowe, was killed by a chance slug from one of the cowhands' guns. So there was two men dead and one hit bad, not to mention Scott being wounded."

"Who were the two cowhands?"

"They were on Mead Guthrie's payroll. There were folks thought they were his bodyguard hired when he heard Scott Fletcher was on the way home. To make a long story short, Scott went to prison for a short term. When the question arose as to ownership of the Fletcher ranch, the court decided in favor of Webb Monroe. On the strength of the bill-of-sale he held with Beriah Fletcher's signature. There it is. How does it look to you, Mr. Quist?"

"What became of the fifty-thousand dollars?"

"Nobody knows. It was never found. The coroner's jury brought in a verdict that Beriah Fletcher had been killed by some Tonkawa Indians. And robbed. Here's something else. After things were settled, Webb Monroe sold the Rafter-F to Mead Guthrie. I ask again, how does it look to you?"

Quist scowled. "I'd guess there'd been some damnable business going on, if I've got the whole story."

"Don't take my word for it. Go up to Tourmaline and talk to Scott Fletcher. Talk to others too."

"Maybe I'll do that. I don't know about Fletcher though. I came through there yesterday, and he wasn't any too cordial. He might take a notion to gun me if I went back."

Hooper shook his head. "Not Scott. He won't gun you."

"You seem right certain."

"Certain I'm certain. Scott won't gun you for the simple reason he doesn't use a gun, refuses to wear one."

"That's hard to believe."

"All right, talk to him yourself. Maybe he can make you understand—though if I was Scott I'd figure I might be taking chances."

There was a thoughtful frown on Quist's face as he finished his beer. "I think I will talk to him myself, Keg. Right now, I've got some other business. I'll see you later."

VI

Webb Monroe was already waiting, seated in one of the row of chairs that lined the gallery railing. Quist dropped into a chair at his side. "Sorry if I've kept you waiting, Monroe. I guess I lingered too long over my drink."

"I know how it is. You get to talking to a customer or maybe the bartender, and before you know it, the time's gone. Take that Keg Cooper. He'll talk the arm off a man if he gets a chance." Monroe paused. "Did he have anything much to say?"

"About what?"

"Oh—" Monroe shrugged his shoulders. "Just things in general. What do barkeeps usually talk about?"

"I've found they listen, mostly—customers' troubles with wives or sweethearts or mothers-in-law.

Female trouble of one sort or another. What was it you wanted to see me about?"

"Deputy Crawford happened to mention last evening that you'd found a skeleton and an old bow and some other stuff up in the mountains yesterday."

Quist chuckled. "Now don't tell me that was your skeleton?"

Monroe looked at him, then laughed rather feebly. "No, I lay no claim to it. But I am interested in the old bow, though."

"You wouldn't be if you had a look at it. I figured it would snap if anybody tried to string it. It's awfully old and the weather has ruined it. I tell you what, I heard someplace that there's a fellow named Fletcher up at Tourmaline who makes bows. I was thinking, if you want a bow, why don't you get him to make you one—?"

"Dammit!" Monroe sounded irritable. "You don't understand. I don't want a bow to shoot. Besides, that's the Fletcher I mentioned last night and he and I don't get along."

Quist pretended not to understand. He shook his head. "Well, if you don't want a bow to shoot, what's the use of getting one? What else can you do with them?"

"Look here, you don't understand. I just want that particular bow—" He broke off, then realized he was being kidded. "What's so damn funny?"

"Could it be that your little boy lost it down by the creek, and you want to get it back for him and you don't want me to break the little tyke's heart for want of an old bow?" Quist chuckled.

Monroe finally got the drift. A sheepish grin touched his lips. "That was a hell of a stupid thing to do, wasn't it?"

"You admit to putting Daulton up to it?"

"Lord, no! Daulton was standing near when Jeff Crawford told me about you finding the bow. Brose Daulton is a right good worker, but sometimes he gets overeager to please. He heard me tell Jeff I'd like to have the bow, so Brose immediately set out to get it in his own way. I knew nothing about it."

"Nor about putting him on my tail, later last night, I suppose," Quist put in.

"That something else I want to talk to you about. Naturally Brose wasn't following you. It just happened he was going the same direction you were, and you jumped to conclusions. He told me what happened. I figure you were sort of rough on the poor cuss. Actually I was riled that one of my men would be treated that way, but I can understand your mistake—"

"I didn't make any mistake."

Spots of angry red burned in Monroe's cheeks. After a minute he gained control of himself. "There's no use arguing about a difference of opinion," he stated in stiff tones. "Let's drop the matter."

"All right, let's. Let's get down to cases. Daulton offered ten dollars for the bow. What's your figure?" Quist's tones were crisp.

"I'll give you twenty," Monroe snapped, "though

it's not worth it. But I'm willing to pay for what I want."

"How do you know it's not worth it until you've seen it? That's where I've got the edge on you. I've actually handled it. Right now, I figure it's worth more than twenty." That was a shot in the dark.

Monroe looked concerned. "What gives you that idea?"

Quist smiled confidently. "The quick way you raised Daulton's price. I'll bet you'll go even higher."

"Damned if I will!" Monroe said furiously. He jerked up and away from his chair. Abruptly, he turned back. "I'm sorry, Mr. Quist. I shouldn't have got mad. You're right, I might go a little higher, but not much."

"Just why are you so anxious to buy that old bow?"

"Why are you so anxious to hang on to it?"

"That's a good question," Quist laughed. "Why am I?"

Monroe looked his exasperation. "Let's cut out this damned niffnawing. Maybe it will sound foolish to you, but I want that bow for my collection. You see—"

"Collection?"

"Collection of artifacts. You see, I'm interested in old Indian relics and Indian history of these parts—"

"You are?" Quist suddenly looked interested, too.

"—and I've been collecting things for years. I've got some flint arrowheads and some ancient clay pots and—and—well, when I've nothing better to do I enjoy studying them. You've no idea how interesting—"

"Damned if this isn't a coincidence." Quist was

49

smiling broadly. He put out one hand. "Shake, brother collector."

Monroe took his hand uncertainly. "You—you mean you're interested in Indian relics too?"

Quist nodded. "Now you know why I want to hang on to that bow. If you ever get to El Paso, look me up and I'll show you my collection. I've got several obsidian arrowheads, and an old lancehead that somebody said was made of jade. It's going to make you jealous to see some of the metates I've got—"

"Metates?"

"You know, the Indians used to grind corn in 'em. I've got 'em all sizes. And then you'll want to see my fossil shells—shucks, Monroe, now you can understand why I don't want to sell that bow."

"We-ell, yes, but, look here, Quist, every man has his price—"

"You'd have to go pretty high, Monroe—" Quist broke off, then, "Look here, I've got an idea. Let's saddle up and ride out to your place. I'd like to see your collection. What do you say?"

Monroe didn't look too enthusiastic. "I can't say I've got time today—"

"Tomorrow, then? I'm plumb anxious to see what you've got."

"To tell the truth, all my stuff is stored in boxes, in one of the barns. They're covered with dust and it would take some time to uncover 'em. I tell you, I'll get 'em set up one of these days before you leave— how long do you expect to be here?"

"Hard to say," Quist replied. "There's one or two things I've got to settle. Railroad business, you understand,"

"Yes, of course. Excuse me a minute, I've got to get a cigar." Looking somewhat angry, Monroe rose and entered the hotel bar.

Quist chuckled. "Him and his collection. What a liar! Maybe there's two liars here, at that. Good thing I went through a museum that time. Artifacts! I'll bet he wouldn't know an artifact from a hole in the ground. But what's so important about that bow? One thing is sure, Monroe doesn't dare go too high in his bidding for fear of arousing my suspicions. But, suspicions of what?"

He broke off his ponderings as Monroe returned, puffing a cigar, and sat down opposite Quist on the gallery railing. "I've been thinking you might have some mistaken notion about the worth of that bow, Quist. What sort of markings were on it?"

Quist grinned insolently at him. "Suppose some sort of old map was scratched into the wood, showing the directions to a lost gold mine—"

"There was?" —eagerly.

"I didn't say that. You were just trying to pump me a mite with your question. So long as you're willing to bid for that bow, I'd be a jackass to tell you anything about it. I'll say one thing, to me it looks mighty interesting."

"Tell me why?"

"What's your next offer?"

Monroe said, "Oh, hell," and turned, sending his gaze out to the street, as though the subject was closed. A few people moved along on the sidewalk; a woman passed carrying a sun parasol and market basket; a cowhand tooled his buckboard to a spot at the general store hitchrack, then jumped down and entered the post office.

A big man with hulking shoulders and grizzled gray hair came up on the gallery. Quist was reminded of a grizzly bear walking on its hind legs. Monroe said, "Morning, Mead. Mead, come over here. Shake hands with Greg Quist, the railroad detective. You've heard about him. Quist, this is Mead Guthrie. Mead runs the Bench-G."

Guthrie extended one hamlike hand in a perfunctory handshake. "Yeah, I heard you were here. Figure you're just wasting your time, Quist. There's no crime around here to speak of. Sheriff Beadle keeps the boys in line, you bet."

Quist said quietly, "Any way it's *my* time that's wasted, and you won't have to pay for it, Guthrie."

"Ain't so sure about that, Quist. Your road's rates are climbing all the time. Got a half-notion to start drivin' my herds through like we did in the old days." Guthrie suddenly laughed. "You and me might get friendly yet—but I don't like cops, and if you ain't a cop of a sort, I'll eat my Stet hat. What you expecting to do here anyway?"

"Right now I've been refusing Monroe's offers for an old bow I found."

"Bow? Injun bow? Webb, what in God's good name do you want an Injun bow for?"

"It's for his collection of artifacts," Quist explained gravely.

"His collection of what?" Guthrie exploded skeptically.

"You know, Mead." Monroe looked nervous. "My collection of relics—Indian relics—historical pieces—"

"Haw-ww-w!" Guthrie's scornful laughter almost made the rafters of the gallery roof ring, startling passersby. "Collection of relics! Buffalo chips! Webb, it wouldn't be hard for me to imagine you collecting another man's cows, but not Injun relics. What you trying to put over on Quist?"

Monroe said in sullen tones. "Not a thing. It's just as I said. I made Quist an offer and he turned it down."

"Then raise it, you damned fool. Never yet saw the man that didn't have his price. What you quibbling about? Quist, what was his offer?"

"Twenty."

"Cents?"

"Dollars."

Guthrie scowled. "Twenty dollars for an old Injun bow? Webb must have been eating loco weed—" He broke off, the scowl deepening. Jerking out a half plug of tobacco, he considered it from all sides, then clamped powerful jaws on a bite. He chewed meditatively for a few moments, then spat a long accurate brown stream at a yellow cat slinking along the

53

roadway at the edge of the sidewalk. The cat emitted a startled yowl, leaped two feet in the air and fled. Guthrie snapped, "I'll give you thirty for the bow, Quist."

"What do you want it for?"

"Ain't got the least idea. Don't know anything about the damn bow, but if Monroe is willing to pay that much, he thinks it is worth it and more. Monroe ain't no fool when it comes to making a quick dollar, so I figure to horn in on the bidding,"

"Hell, let's drop the subject," Monroe said testily.

"You interested in thirty, Quist?" Guthrie demanded.

"The bow's not for sale at present," Quist said.

"Think over my offer. It will be eventually," Guthrie said confidently. He swung on Monroe. "What I wanted to see you about Webb, was that stamp-iron stock you said you'd sell me. I been waiting a week now. My blacksmith ain't got much to do and now's the time to hammer out some new brand irons."

"Didn't figure you'd want it until spring when calf round-up was due. Sure that stock is in the barn. I'll have one of the boys ride over with it—"

"It's probably holding down the boxes Monroe's artifacts are in," Quist said, rising from his chair. "I warn you, Guthrie, it may take a few days to get 'em out."

Monroe glared at him. Guthrie frowned but didn't say anything. Quist gave the two men a brief nod, said, "See you again, gents," and sauntered down to the sidewalk.

He started east along Trail Street, keeping on the shady side. "Now was that an act Guthrie staged, or doesn't he really know anything about that bow?"

VII

As he was about to pass the sheriff's office, Quist glanced inside and saw Beadle at his desk. He crossed the porch on a sudden impulse and stepped inside the office. Beadle glanced around, then swung in his swivel chair to face Quist.

"Mornin'. Grab a chair, Mr. Quist."

"Make it Greg."

"I'll do that. My first name's Mort—really Morton. What's on your mind?"

"Just thought I'd drop in and say much obliged for the work you did for the T.N. & A.S."

"What was that?"

"Those freight thieves that stole the cases of whisky."

"Sho', now. That was nothing. Those two no-goods got drunk enough to do too much talking and Jeff Crawford just naturally picked 'em up. Didn't amount to much. That sort of crime don't. Now, I imagine you find more interesting cases."

"Some of 'em yes, some, no. It's a job like anything else. Keeps me traveling around a lot. Sometimes I wish I could stay in one place." Quist glanced around the office. "I suppose that cot against the wall is Jeff Crawford's."

"Mine. Jeff has a room over on Atacosa Street. I just figure a sheriff should be on duty day and night, in case anybody needs him fast. Ain't had anything of that sort for a long spell though. And Jeff handles most of the trouble that comes up, anyway."

"Good man, eh?"

"Jeff's all right." Beadle didn't sound too enthusiastic.

"Been with you long?"

"Close to four years. He had a job as deputy in Puma County when he came here to pick up a prisoner one time. I liked his looks, and offered him a job here. I was needing a deputy at the time. I'd just lost one through an accident. Good man named Stowe."

"Accident?"

Beadle frowned. He didn't appear too anxious to talk of the matter, but briefly explained, "We had a little gun flurry in town. One of the shots went wild and dropped Stowe as he ran in to stop it."

"Would that be the Scott Fletcher business?"

"Somebody been telling you about that?" Beadle asked quickly.

"I was having a drink in one of the bars. I beard somebody mention it. Wasn't quite clear to me what it was about."

"Hell, I figured folks had forgot it, long ago. It was sort of too bad. Scott Fletcher's father was murdered by some Injuns, and Scott jumped to the wrong conclusions as to who done it. He started on the warpath to avenge his father, ready to throw lead at a couple of beef raisers here. I tried to talk sense into him, but it was no good. Had my deputy, Stowe, set to stop things too. But things happened too fast to be stopped. Scott was convicted and served time. He was lucky to get off as easy as he did."

"How come?"

"We-ell," Beadle said reluctantly, "there was some conflicting evidence as to who shot first. I guess the judge thought Scott Fletcher deserved the benefit of the doubt, having just lost his father. I figured Scott was in the wrong, but . . ." Beadle's voice trailed off as though reluctant to continue the subject.

Quist allowed the matter to drop. The two men idly discussed town matters, the price of beef, railroad vs. stage travel. Quist glanced through the open doorway. Directly across Trail Street stood a large frame building with wide closed doors. Across its high false-front was painted: Rosebud Theatre. On the other corner, on the same side of the street as the Rosebud, was located the War-Drum Saloon. A number of men were lounging at the tierail and indulging in some horse-play and rough jokes, talking in loud voices and laughing a great deal. All wore cowpuncher togs. Passersby were forced to go out to the road to get past them.

Quist suddenly rose from his chair and went to the open doorway. He said shortly, "Vink Fisher."

"What about him? You know him?" The sheriff left his seat and stood at Quist's shoulder.

"Yes, I know him. I didn't know he was out of the penitentiary, though. He was serving a term for killing a man in a gunfight in Jack Harris's gambling house in San 'Tonia. Had an idea he was fast with a gun. And proved it, the way things turned out for the other man."

Beadle looked concerned. "I'll bet Webb Monroe doesn't know that. Fisher's not been here long."

"He's on Monroe's payroll?"

Beadle nodded. "All those fellers are. Damned if I understand why Webb keeps such a rough-tough gang in his crew. It ain't like him. And every time he's in town, they come with him. I sometimes wonder when any ranch work gets done."

"Maybe Monroe feels he needs a bodyguard."

Beadle looked startled. "Why should he need a bodyguard?"

"He had trouble with Fletcher once, didn't he? Maybe Monroe figures Fletcher hasn't forgotten it."

Beadle looked troubled. He said after a minute, "Those hombres over there will rough-house around like that in fun, until some man will refuse to get off the sidewalk for them. Then the first thing you know there'll be a real fight started." He stepped out to the porch, raised his voice, "Hey, you hombres, quiet down! Behave yourselves! You hear me?"

Quist talked to the sheriff a moment or two longer, then stepped out to the street. Nearly a block away, he saw Crawford heading west on Trail Street. Watching a few seconds more, he noted that the deputy turned in at the Inwood Hotel. Quist shrugged his shoulders and going by way of Caddo Street, ended up at the T.N. & A.S. station. Here he again produced his credentials for the benefit of the day stationmaster and sent a telegram to Jay Fletcher, after warning the man the wire was confidential. Lane Johnson, the regular station man, wasn't due to come on until twelve noon.

Quist was about to leave when the station man said, "A telegram just arrived for you, Mr. Quist." Quist accepted the paper the man pushed through the grilled window. It proved to be from the Superintendent of Divisions, in answer to the note Quist had sent the previous evening, and read,

YOUR NOSE FOR TROUBLE APPEARS STILL IN WORKING CONDITION. MAN IN QUESTION DISTANT RELATION. NOT KNOW PERSONALLY. OWNS FIVE SHARES COMPANY STOCK. STAY ON JOB.

JAY FLETCHER.

Quist folded the telegram and put it in his pocket, chuckling, "I think I'd like to know more about Mr. Scott Fletcher." Consulting his watch he saw it was getting along toward eleven o'clock. "But I'd best grab a quick bite first."

He followed the tracks until he reached Crockett Street and then turned toward Trail, where he'd remembered seeing a Mexican restaurant. Here he stoked his appetite with a large bowl of chili, *tortillas,* hot peppers and coffee. His mouth burning from the peppers, he decided to get a beer before saddling his horse. He was about to turn into the hotel, when Jeff

Crawford hailed him from across the street. Quist waited at the edge of the sidewalk, until Crawford had crossed over.

"I've been looking for you, Greg," the deputy said.

"What have I done now?" Quist smiled. "Am I under arrest? If so, give me time to get a beer first."

Crawford laughed. "It's not that serious. Look here, the sheriff wants that bow."

Quist sobered. "How come?"

"Well," Crawford explained awkwardly, "we got to thinking it over—and, that is, Mort was thinking about it—and he decided we'd better investigate that skeleton you found. In case it does turn out important, he feels he should have that bow as evidence."

Quist frowned, thinking, Somebody sure brought pressure to bear on Beadle in a hurry. Monroe? Guthrie? Aloud, he said, "Mort changed his mind in a hurry, didn't he?"

"It sort of looks that way, Greg. It won't take you a minute to get it. Sorry to bother you—you see how it is—"

"I'm not sure I do, Jeff," Quist said flatly. "What's queer about that bow is that it's so popular all of a sudden. Monroe tried to buy it this morning. Then Guthrie, and—"

"Guthrie?" Crawford looked startled.

"You don't seem surprised that Monroe tried to buy it."

"I'm not," Crawford said quickly. "You see, Webb has a collection of old—"

"Old buffalo chips," Quist cut in scornfully. "Don't tell me he handed you that line of talk too?"

Crawford shrugged his shoulders. "All I know is what he told me, Greg. I don't want to make any hard feelings, but we've got to have that bow. Mort says so."

"You can tell Mort he's going to be disappointed."

"I wish you wouldn't act that way, Greg." Crawford shifted uneasily. "We don't want to have any trouble with you, but you know Mort's head boss in this county, where the law's concerned. He'd like to have you surrender the bow peacefully, and that's what he expected you'd do, but—"

"He's going to have his expectations changed," Quist said shortly. "I found that bow. And the skeleton. The sheriff wasn't interested in either, last night. All right, finders, keepers."

"You're making things hard for us, Greg. Can't you see, Mort can simply use his badge, his authority, to make you turn that bow over to him—"

Quist snorted. "He can buck the T.N. & A.S., too, if he wants to make a damned fool of himself. Look, Jeff, face it squarely. Do you honestly think the sheriff is stronger than my company? Who do you think would win in a showdown of power?"

Crawford's gaze was troubled. Finally he replied, "I guess you've got the upper hand, Greg. I admit it. But what am I going to tell Mort when I go back?"

"Tell him what you like," Quist said shortly.

"He'll strip the hide off my bones—"

"The sheriff doesn't look that rough to me."

"You don't know him. He can be hard as nails—look, you can get me off the hook, if you'll come and explain things to Mort yourself. Would you do that?"

"Why not?" Quist shrugged and the two men started for the sheriff's office. The office was empty when they arrived. "Mort must have gone to dinner early," Crawford observed. "He should be back in a short spell."

"Meanwhile, I've got to have a bottle of beer. I ate some peppers at the Mexican's a spell back, and I've got a hunch he stuffed them with hot coals. My mouth is on fire."

"Let's go across to the War-Drum while we're waiting."

Quist nodded and they crossed diagonally to the saloon, which stood on the corner. It was dim and cool within, after the sunglare of Trail Street, and it took a moment for Quist to adjust his eyes to the change of light. By that time he and Crawford had bottles of beer before them. Quist took several swallows and then glanced around. The bar ran from rear to front at one side and was presided over by a beetle-browed barkeep. There were several men at the far end of the bar, and Quist noticed they were the same ones who'd been roughhousing it out in front some time before.

"What is this, the Monroe outfit hangout?" Quist asked.

"More or less," the deputy nodded. He took another

drink of beer. "Those boys get right playful on occasion and Mort or I have to quiet 'em down."

Vink Fisher, a lean swarthy man with stringy black hair hanging over his forehead and a battered holster and gun hanging at his hip, broke away from the group and came down the bar.

"How's it going, Quist?"

"About as usual, Fisher." Quist was still bellied up to the bar, but turned his head to address the man. "How long you been out?"

Fisher scowled then forced a wide grin. "Not so loud. You'll ruin my rep 'round here."

"That I doubt," Quist said shortly. "I asked a question."

"Six months, more or less."

"You got off easy, considering you were tried for murder."

"Murder wasn't never proved. I was put on by that feller, and he forced me to shoot. I always regretted it too. Nights in my cell I'd dwell on what I'd done to a fellow man, and the thought fair made me shiver. I got so I was plumb horror struck—"

"Bosh!" Quist snorted.

"Don't be like that, Quist," Fisher complained. "I really repented, learned to lead a Christian life, and the God-Shouter helped me to read the Bible and explained things—"

"So you pulled the wool over the chaplain's eyes," Quist cut in.

"—and I attended services on Sunday mornings—"

"You might fool a prison chaplain, Fisher. I don't swallow that guff."

"Look, Quist, just because a man made a mistake—"

"It should learn him not to make another."

"Gesis, Quist, you act like you don't want to be friends. I'm trying to tell you. I got paroled for good behavior—"

"You never knew what the word meant, Fisher," Quist said bluntly. "And no, I'm not interested in being friends. I wouldn't dare trust you. If I'd been on your case, you'd stayed in a cell until the ants carried you out through the keyhole."

Fisher's swarthy face flushed as one of his companions heard the remark. "Still posing as a hard hombre, eh, Quist? One of these days you're going to get your comeuppance."

"Not from you, Vink. You lack nerve to try anything." Quist smiled scornfully and moved one thumb across the mouth of his beer bottle. Idly he rocked the bottle back and forth, one eye on Fisher and the other keeping watch on the reflections in the backbar. The Monroe men were all watching eagerly to see what would take place.

"The time will come, lawman, when I'll show you how much nerve I've got. You think you're a little tin-god on wheels and can rough folks up as much as you like, but you're due to be stopped one of these days—"

"Not by a scut like you, Fisher." Quist took a firmer grip on the bottle, feeling the pressure building against his thumb, and rocked it casually. "If you were really tough, you'd be reaching for your gun now. But your nerve's petering out. Your rep won't be worth a damn with your pards." Someone snickered loudly.

"God damn you, Quist!" Fisher backed away a step, face flaming, trying to summon sufficient courage to draw his gun. He'd never intended things to go this far, but goaded by laughter at his rear, he lost his head. "Maybe you're asking for it," he snarled, hand dropping toward his gun. "We'll see—"

Quist moved his right arm, turned the mouth of the bottle toward Fisher and released his thumb from the opening. With the charged violence of a jet from a fire-hose, the pent-up, gassy suds spurted a white foaming deluge full into Fisher's angry face.

Fisher staggered back, mouthing obscene oaths, clawing at his eyes with one hand while the other fumbled for a bandanna. Laughing, Quist released another shower of gas-charged suds, drenching Fisher's face and shirt. Howls of laughter rose from the Monroe men. Quist stepped forward, snatching the gun from Fisher's holster. The now-empty bottle he tossed to the floor at Fisher's feet. Fisher's stumbling step landed on the bottle. It rolled under foot and the man abruptly crashed down in a puddle of beer.

"You're not worth wasting a ca'tridge on, Fisher," Quist said contemptuously, as he started toward the street followed by Crawford.

"Vink Fisher got so much religion when he was in the pen," Quist grinned, "that I decided to hold baptismal services for the boys. Here's his gun, Crawford.

Give it back to him when he gets some sense in his thick noggin—"

Quist didn't wait for the sheriff's return but headed down the street to his hotel. At the desk he got some old newspapers and twine and continued up to his room, closing the door behind him. Once in the room he picked up the old bow and studied it for a few minutes.

"There's just too many people wanting to get their hands on this bow, all of a sudden," he grunted testily, and looked about the room for something to take its place.

He considered removing a length of one of the chairs for a moment, then discarded the idea. His gaze went to the rolled shades at the window and dismissed that thought. He wanted lowered shades in his room when he had the light on. Finally he strode to the dresser and yanked out an empty lower drawer. Not quite long enough, but he might make it do. The backing piece of wood wasn't too heavy, and had been assembled to the drawer with light nails. Quist gripped the drawer and exerted his strength. The nails began to loosen. Another muscular jerk and the board came loose from the drawer.

It was of pine and looked as though it would split easily. Quist drew out his Barlow knife and a minute later had split off two lengths of the board, a couple of inches wide. Next he spread out some newspapers, and carefully arranging the pine strips, quickly rolled them in several thickness of newspaper. That done, the

66

package was neatly tied with twine and placed on the floor against one wall.

"Anyway," he considered, "I'm the only one who knows how long the bow is. But how in the devil am I to get the how out of here without being seen?"

He stood frowning a minute in the center of the floor, then went to his side window and flung it open. People pursued the course of their business along Trail Street. Just below, along Deming, there were no pedestrians. Quist hoped that condition would continue. He studied the shingled roof of the gallery which sloped sharply just a few inches from the bottom of his window until it reached a galvanized gutter which extended above the sidewalk. Stepping back into his room, Quist got the bow and returned to the open window. He placed the bow, end down, on the gallery roof and gave it a shove. It slid slowly, but directly, end on, until it came to a stop at the gutter where it lay still. Quist glanced about. Apparently no one had taken notice of his movements.

He withdrew his head, closed the window. A minute later he had descended the stairs and was crossing Trail to the Flying Hooves Livery. Here he got his saddled horse, climbed into the saddle and once more emerged on the street. "Luck's with me so far," he mused. "Nobody in the lobby but the clerk, though he might have told someone if he'd seen me come out with the bow."

He glanced along the gallery. No one occupied the row of chairs along the railing at the moment. Casually, Quist headed the pony in a diagonal direction toward the hotel corner, but instead of straightening it out when he reached Deming Street, he guided it up on the sidewalk following the course of the gallery at the side. Now he could almost reach up and touch the gallery roof gutter. As he drew nearer, he rose slightly in his stirrups, fingers of one hand fumbling along the gutter until they encountered the end of the bow. Then he lifted it quickly from its resting place, and settled back to his saddle. A quick glance over his shoulder told him that, apparently, no one had seen anything.

He reined the buckskin to the middle of Deming Street and continued at a walk, north, until he'd reached Atacosa Street, which paralleled Trail. Here he turned left and put the horse to a swift lope, musing, "Well, the bait is there. We'll see if anyone wants it bad enough to come after it."

VIII

The buckskin pushed steadily on. It grew warmer as the sun mounted. Quist mopped at his forehead with a bandanna. "Whoever it was said that Tourmaline was only five or six miles from Horcado City must have been talking about as the crow flies. By the time you've cut over this far to where the trail climbs, it must be farther—particularly when you've made said climb."

Off to his right he spied a bunch of white-faced Herefords being pushed toward the creek by a rider on a chestnut horse. The cows were branded on the right hip with the Bench-G design. The cowhand raised one hand in a casual salute to Quist; Quist replied with a similar motion and pushed on past. Once he slowed the buckskin for a 'breather,' while he twisted a Durham cigarette. The smoke finished, he stubbed out the fire on his saddlehorn, touched spurs to the horse's ribs and moved into a faster pace, the loping hoofs raising small flurries of dust at the rear which were lifted and swept to invisibility by the steadily blowing breeze.

Gradually, horse and man were climbing, negotiating the trail where it ran between low foothills. The rocky granite bluffs were far above his head now, though nearer at hand were clumps of cedar and post oak. Abruptly, the way swerved to the left, growing somewhat steeper and showing plainly the marks of wheels and horses' hoofs. Mountain juniper grew on either side.

The way leveled off as he reached a wide plateau. Just ahead now, with a turn to the left, would be Tourmaline. Trees at either side obscured view of the buildings as yet. Again he slowed the buckskin to maneuver his way around a great block of granite the size of a two-story house. Then just as he was about to leave the trees for the more open stretch of Tourmaline, something flew swiftly past his eyes and he heard a sharp thud some distance to his right. Whatever the flying missile, it was too far ahead to have been intended to hit him.

Quist pulled to a sudden halt and blinked his eyes. What in the devil had it been? Had he really seen something, the swift flight of a small bird perhaps, or was it all imagination? There came a sharp twanging sound. Again he received the same blurred sensation of something having passed across his line of vision, followed instantly by a second sharp thud, as though some hidden knife-thrower had hurled his pointed blade into some slightly resisting object.

Things abruptly cleared for Quist. Arrows! He raised his voice: "I'm coming in! Hold your fire!"

No one answered, though Quist caught the sound of voices and moving feet. Then, a girl's tones, slightly louder. "I will not hurry, Scott. I'm tired of hiding—" And the man's voice: "It may make more trouble—" And the girl's again, stubborn: "I don't give a hoot! I can face it. . . ."

Quist urged the buckskin to a walk, lowered his head as they passed beneath a low-hanging limb, and found himself on Tourmaline's weed-cluttered street, the dilapidated old buildings lined up before him. Directly in the middle of the street, before the white-washed building he'd noticed on his previous visit, stood a scowling Scott Fletcher and a girl with great masses of rich auburn hair piled high on her head. She wore a green corduroy divided skirt, riding boots and a mannish flannel shirt, open at the throat; her sleeves were rolled above the elbows. On her left arm was a sort of leather armband, and on the right hand she wore a three-fingered glove which covered only the tips of fingers. She was holding a strung bow, as tall as herself, and Fletcher gripped a handful of arrows. Her felt sombrero had been tossed on the earth to one side.

Quist realized suddenly that she had been shooting at the target he'd noticed when he'd been here before. It stood some 60 or 75 yards distant, fastened to the high stack of straw bales, with the branches of a great live oak overhanging the bales. The target already had several arrows protruding from its surface, though there were none in the bull's-eye.

Scott Fletcher looked worried. There was a frown on his forehead, his gray eyes had narrowed. Finally, as Quist drew to a halt a short distance away, Fletcher said, "Howdy, what can I do for you?"

Quist removed his hat. "I'm not sure, yet. I'm Gregory Quist. I wanted to talk to you a mite."

Fletcher's brow cleared a little, and the girl cut in, "Scott, please ask the man to step down. He doesn't look as though he'd bite, or anything."

"By all means," Fletcher said hurriedly. "You—you're the railroad detective I heard was in Horcado City." He forced a thin smile. "I assure you I've not been impeding T.N. & A.S. business in any way—oh, yes, Mr. Quist, this is Sheila Guthrie. Sheila, Mr. Quist seems to have Horcado City quite stirred up."

Quist stepped down from the saddle and bowed to the girl and said he was more than pleased to meet her, wondering at the same time if she were any relation to Mead Guthrie.

As though guessing what was passing through his mind, Sheila Guthrie said, "Yes, I'm Mead Guthrie's daughter," and gave Quist her gloved hand. She turned to Fletcher, "Remember, Scott, he's got that bow Dad tried to buy." She explained to Quist, "I was talking to Dad in town just before I rode up here. He's puzzled as to what's so precious about your old bow."

"I'm hoping Mr. Fletcher may throw some light on the subject," Quist replied.

"I was just giving Sheila a few pointers in archery," Fletcher explained, "but—"

"Go right ahead," Quist said. "I'm in no hurry. My business may take a little time. And just to relieve your mind, I'm not accusing you of any crimes against the railroad."

He drew the horse to one side and then turned it. Fletcher said suddenly, "That bow on the saddle. Is that the one Sheila said her father wanted to buy from you?"

"That's it." Quist got the bow and handed it to the young man. Fletcher examined it with keen interest. He looked sharply at Quist. "If you want to have this put in good shape, I doubt it can be done, Mr. Quist. It's been out in too many kinds of weather too many times. I might be able to take it down and make a lighter bow, but—" He broke off suddenly, as be scrutinized the bow near the middle, then glanced sharply at Quist.

Quist asked, "Discover something interesting?"

Fletcher didn't reply at once, then said slowly, "Oh,

no, it's just a well-made bow. Good workmanship. It's made from osage wood. Did I hear that you'd found it?"

Quist nodded. Fletcher said, "I want to hear more about it."

"That's why I'm up here. Maybe we can put two and two together. Keg Hooper mentioned that he didn't think you'd had a square deal one time—"

"Oh, Keg—he's a good friend."

"What he said interested me. I've heard various stories about you from different people. I wanted to hear your side of it. I'm curious that way."

"It may take some time."

"That I have plenty of. Go ahead with what you and Miss Guthrie were doing. I can wait."

"That's good. You'd better put your horse in the corral. You'll find water—oh, yes, of course, you didn't know. The corral's down back of those straw bales. Just ahead on down past that big oak. You can't miss it. We'll hold our fire until you get back."

Quist nodded, picked up his reins and led the horse away, musing, "So now you two can get together on your stories if necessary and decide what to do with me—if necessary. But what's Guthrie's daughter doing up here? And what was the talk about hiding? As I got it, Guthrie was an enemy of Fletcher's."

Forehead furrowed with thought, Quist made his way around one end of the stacked bales and passed beneath the big oak tree. Here the way slanted down somewhat to a small hollow, surrounded by junipers, and a moment later he saw the bars of the pole corral, near the gate of which stood a wagon. There were four horses in the corral, one of which, a small chestnut gelding, he assumed belonged to Sheila Guthrie. There was a well-filled drinking trough, and after Quist had taken care of the buckskin and rubbed down its back beneath the saddle, he made his way back to Tourmaline's street, where the other two awaited him.

The bow Quist had brought was nowhere in sight. At the edge of the road lay two other bows, and by this time Fletcher wore on his back a doeskin quiver full of arrows. As Quist joined them, Fletcher said, "Go ahead, Sheila."

"Considering that target is four feet wide," the girl stated, "I should do better. I did get a red 7, once, today," she explained to Quist.

"You've been shooting too long," Fletcher said. "You'd better stop pretty soon."

But the girl had already taken another arrow and was placing it on her bow. Fletcher watched her narrowly as she raised the bow. "Keep that left shoulder toward the target—turn your head, not your body. Now, draw easily. Don't loose until I say so. No, your hand is too far back. Straighten out that left arm a little more. Bring your right hand and the string back until it's just about even with your chin. Easy now. Hold it a minute. Your elbow's too low. No. Now you got it too high. Wait a moment."

He came behind the girl, placing one hand on the bow. His other arm went to her hand pulling back the string. For a moment they stood motionless, his arms around her. Quist speculated that giving archery lessons might be enjoyable.

"Now, you see,"—Fletcher stood back—"your right hand is just where it should be. Straighten your shoulders. Now—release easily." *Twang!* The arrow left the bow, struck the target.

Sheila ejaculated a disappointed, "Shucks! I felt sure I was going to get a gold bull's-eye that time."

"You got a blue 5," Fletcher said. "You jerked slightly on your release. When you loose, just straighten your fingers easy. Don't worry, you'll get the hang of it." He noticed Sheila rubbing her right arm. "You'd better quit now."

The girl nodded. "Let Mr. Quist try it?"

Quist looked startled. "Me?"

"Why not," Fletcher asked. "I brought out an extra bow." He got the unstrung bow and handed it to Quist. "Ever do this before?"

"Had an Indian bow when I was a kid, like most younkers those days. But it was nothing like this." Quist tried to string the bow and found it required more strength than he'd realized. The string was permanently fastened to one end of the bow; the loop at the other end of the string slid along the bow, but Quist couldn't quite slide it into the notch at the end, and at the same time keep the bow in a bent position. The instant he released his pressure, the bow snapped straight again.

"You're making work of it, Mr. Quist," Fletcher

said. "There's a knack to it that makes it easier. Let me show you."

Placing the bottom end of the bow against the inside of his left foot, with the erect flat side of the bow toward him—the inner side was rounded—Fletcher grasped the bow in the center with his left hand, holding it firm, while he exerted pressure with his right to bend the bow, the right fingers sliding along until they encountered the loop. Now he bent the bow still farther, and his hand easily slipped the loop into its nock at the upper end. The bow was strung. He employed similar methods in unstringing it, and said to Quist. "Try it again."

Quist took the bow and after some further instruction found the stringing came quite easily. Fletcher handed him a three-fingered glove for his right hand, saying, "If you'll take off your coat I can give you an armguard for your left forearm. A string slap can be mighty nasty at times. That glove will save your fingers some too."

Mindful of his underarm gun harness Quist retained his coat. "I don't figure I'll be shooting long enough to use a lot of equipment," he said. "I'll make out as it is."

Further instructions found Quist trying to fit the arrow's nock to the taut bow string, a business that made him feel unusually clumsy and fumble-fingered. The arrow was a slim length of birch more than two feet in length, fitted at one end with feathers and at the other with a blunted brass point. Quist's first few efforts found the arrow falling away from the bow before he could get set to draw. In his boyhood he had been accustomed to grasp the feathered end of the arrow between thumb and forefingers. Now he learned that, once nocked, he was simply to hold the arrow between his first and second fingers, and hooking three fingers about the string, draw it back until the string reached the vicinity of his chin.

It required a half dozen attempts before he succeeded in loosing an arrow that reached the straw bales, though it came nowhere near the target. Quist laughed. "Yesterday I wondered why such a large target was necessary. I think now you'd better paint a target that covers all those bales."

"You'll get it," Fletcher encouraged. A dozen additional tries later and Quist scored a black 3. Fletcher praised him and Sheila clapped her hands. Quist asked, "Can anyone hit that gold bull's-eye consistently?"

"Scott can," Sheila said promptly.

Fletcher colored. "Now, look here, Sheila, you'll give Mr. Quist the idea that I'm better than I really am. If he believes you."

"I'll believe her," Quist said readily, "though I admit I'd like to see it done. I'm a curious hombre at times."

"Show Mr. Quist, Scott," Sheila urged.

Fletcher's cheeks were still a trifle red as he self-consciously strung his bow. He checked the arrows in the quiver hanging at his back, feather end up, though he didn't remove one at the moment. He glanced at the target, left shoulder facing it, gave consideration to the breeze. Then his right. hand flashed back over his shoulder, seized an arrow and fitted it to his bow, his movements unbelievably swift, and loosed it. *Twang—thwap!* as the arrow ripped into the circle adjoining the gold bull's-eye.

"Red seven," Fletcher stated. "See Mr. Quist, I'm not as good as Sheila claimed."

"But, Scott, you were just getting the range," Sheila protested.

Quist's eyes had widened at the speed displayed. "Anyway, it looked right good to me," he conceded.

The words had scarcely left his lips before Fletcher went into action. Arrows were fitted to the string of the bow and released in a seemingly steady stream, Fletcher's movements a fluid blur of swift motion. Only seconds elapsed between each shot.

Twang—thwap! Twang—thwap! Twang—thwap! Twang—thwap! Twang—thwap! Twang—thwap! Before Quist could quite realize it, six arrows had imbedded themselves in the bull's-eye, two near the edge, the feathers of the other four crowding each other.

Quist's jaw dropped. "Good God, that's fast!" he exclaimed. "And accurate! How the deuce do you do it?"

Fletcher smiled, lowering his bow. "Continual daily practice, Mr. Quist. Like's not, you'd do as well with the same amount of shooting."

"That I doubt," Quist stated.

Sheila settled her sombrero on her head, then the three strolled down to the target to retrieve the arrows, Quist thinking, Well, this is one way to study a man. Show an interest in his game and he'll generally thaw some.

They were drawing arrows out of the target now, and Fletcher slipped them into his quiver. Sheila said, "So long as I'm this close to the corral, Scott, I might as well get saddled up and head home. The afternoon is passing fast."

Scott nodded, hesitated a moment, then, "If you like, Mr. Quist, you can go up to my place and get a beer. You won't have any trouble locating the cooler, though I've got no ice."

"That's welcome news." Quist nodded to Sheila. "Hope to see you again, Miss Guthrie." The girl said she hoped so too, and the two disappeared around the corner of the straw bales, while Quist trudged back to the house, chuckling, "Well, Fletcher couldn't have made it any plainer, if he'd said bluntly they wanted to be alone for a few minutes. And she certainly didn't appear reluctant."

IX

Quist paused a minute to look over Fletcher's place, before entering. As he'd noticed previously it was constructed of gray granite blocks, irregular in form, and had recently been whitewashed. The roof was flat with a low parapet along the front. The wall facing the

79

street held two large windows, and between them the door stood slightly ajar.

Quist mounted the three steps to Fletcher's place and pushed on inside. He glanced around. There was only the single large room, with the face of the granite bluff forming the back wall. "The cooler, now where's the cooler?" Quist muttered, before spotting a closed door at the back of the room. He opened the door and commented, "Nice set-up," taking in the small chamber that had been blasted out of the sheer granite wall. There were shelves on both sides, holding various objects. Quist had no trouble locating a case of beer and securing a bottle. He emerged, closing the door of the cooler behind him, and on a shelf found an opener for the bottle.

It was the remainder of the room that held Quist's greater attention. There were two large work benches, one just beneath a front window and one ranged along a side wall, equipped with vises and various other tools necessary to making archery tackle. A glue pot and small cans of various colored paints and varnishes stood at one end. Suspended from individual hooks on the side wall were at least three dozens bows of various types, weights and lengths. Other hooks held bow strings. A row of empty tomato cans, each holding several arrows of various types, was ranged below the bows. Arrow points from the blunt variety to sharp steel broadheads for hunting were carefully sorted in small boxes. Another box held wild turkey, buzzard, and eagle feathers for fletching arrows. Below the bench were bundles of arrow dowels and long wood billets, some with the bark still clinging to one side, ranging in color from pale yellow through orange to red, waiting to be manufactured into bows.

And at the far end of the wall bench rested the bow Quist had brought.

A rattling of arrows in a quiver announced Scott Fletcher's approach. Quist hadn't even heard the girl take her departure. Fletcher entered, closed the door behind him, and tossed his sombrero to a chair seat. "I see you found the beer all right. You look about due for another. I'll join you. Then I'll get supper started."

Ten minutes later leaping flames in the fireplace were lighting the room. Fletcher busied himself with kitchen utensils after making a couple of trips to his cooler. Before long he had a Dutch oven and the coffee pot in place above the flames. "Just as soon as that oak burns down to embers I'll show you some real steaks, Mr. Quist. What? Yes, I really shot the deer myself, with an arrow. I even shot a bear once. And knew a man who downed a grizzly with a single arrow. I took most of the deer meat into Horcado City this morning and sold it. A butcher buys all I can bring in. The extra dollars come handy."

"I don't suppose there is much of a living in five shares of T.N. & A.S. stock," Quist commented.

Fletcher had been setting the table with plates, cups, and utensils. He stopped and looked sharply at Quist. "You have been checking up on me, haven't you?"

"That's part of my business," Quist nodded.

"Why check up on me?" Fletcher demanded.

"Put it down to the fact that I'm curious. I don't mind telling you that I didn't come here to check up on you. One or two things I picked up aroused my interest. Then, too, you're a distant relative of Jay Fletcher, our Superintendent of Divisions. Considering your five shares of stock, it might be said I'm working for you."

The venison steaks, when they arrived at the table, were announced "prime" by Quist. In addition there were sourdough biscuits, stewed canned tomatoes and canned peaches. The coffee was black and heavy the way Quist liked it. "Scott Fletcher, you're more than a cook—you're a real chef." Quist leaned back and patted his belly. "If you ever give up this bow-and-arrow game I'll be glad to recommend you to some hotel kitchen."

"Thanks," Fletcher smiled, "but I'll stick to archery for the present."

"Quite a set-up you have here."

Fletcher shrugged. "I get by on what I make. And it's enjoyable work. I receive orders for tackle from many people in the East."

Fletcher placed fresh wood on the fire and returned to the table with the coffee pot. There was a certain chill in the night air and the fireplace heated well. Quist removed his coat. Fletcher mentioned the underarm gun and holster, while he was pouring coffee.

"That's quite a harness you've got there."

"Best I've been able to devise to date."

"But what keeps the gun from falling out?"

"A metal spring enclosed in the leather. This way instead of reaching down to the holster and then lifting the gun, losing a second or so, I just reach across and the butt of my forty-four is practically in my hand. As I draw it, it's already level for shooting. And a second saved in getting my gun into action may make a big difference."

"But you don't wear any ca'tridge belt."

"I carry a few extras in my coat pocket. Any man that can't do his job with that many ca'tridges hasn't any business carrying a gun. And I'm relieved of the weight of a ca'tridge belt."

They settled to Durham cigarettes and coffee. Fletcher said, "Maybe it would be better, Mr. Quist, if you'd tell me just what you've heard about me, before I tell my version."

"Not a bad idea." Quist related the various stories he'd picked up. When he had concluded, Fletcher said, frowning, "Some of it is a mite biased, I'd say, but in the main I guess you heard the truth as some people see it. But you didn't get all the truth. In the first place you didn't learn what caused the trouble between Mead Guthrie and my Dad."

Quist shook his head. "I knew Beriah Fletcher once owned the Rafter-F Ranch. It was later sold to Webb Monroe and now Guthrie runs it under the Bench-G iron."

"Dad was going to revolutionize the Tonkawas'

weapons. But they would have none of it. They wanted firearms, not archery tackle. Dad never made but one convert and that was a Tonkawa named Niquatonne—Dad called him Nick. Nick had a higher intelligence than the other Tonkawas—and realized that Dad was genuinely interested in helping him. He took to Dad's kind of bow and when he could shoot well, Dad made one for him. The two of them used to hunt regularly. Matter of fact, he was like Dad's shadow. Followed him everywhere. When the other Tonkawas sort of faded away, Nick stayed at the ranch with Dad."

"That's when you got started hunting with arrows?"

Fletcher's face clouded. "No, I wish to God I had. Sometimes I think that Nick, the Tonkawa, was a better son than I was. Dad was a sort of gentle man, who tried to avoid trouble. He had a lot of sense too, and when he saw me feeling my oats and getting into scrapes in town, he shipped me off for some schooling. Well, I didn't like schools, either. Nor did I want to stay on a ranch all my life. I fooled around with archery somewhat, but I had a wandering foot and wouldn't stay put. I was all for developing into a fast gun, too, and that didn't set well with Dad. Actually I was too fast for my own good, though I never got into any real bad scrapes until later. So that's the way it went. I'd attend some school for a time and then come back and get into another jam, then off to another school. I wasn't a good student, but some of it stuck with me."

"What *was* your father's trouble with Mead Guthrie?"

"It started one time after calf round-up was finished, and Guthrie found some calves branded with our Rafter-F following Bench-G cows. Lord knows how it happened. Dad was the last man in the world to steal another man's cows, or brand his calves. All we could think of was that there'd been somebody careless when the branding was done, or the wrong brand had been called out. Well, Guthrie had been missing a lot of cows and he jumped to conclusions. He accused Dad of rustling. Dad denied it. Guthrie blew wide open and announced no man was going to call him a liar, and he challenged Dad to draw. Dad refused. I wanted to take up the fight, but Dad shut me up. I was just at the age when I was ready to jump into a gun-fight. That started the trouble and from then on Dad and Guthrie were enemies."

"You have any idea who might have been running off Guthrie's stock?"

"Yes, I had an idea, but no proof. Personally, I figured that Webb Monroe was responsible. He'd come here with practically nothing and the first thing everybody knew was that he had a going outfit. You'd think his cows were having calves by the litter."

Quist considered. "It wouldn't be easy to change a Bench-G or a Rafter-F to a Diamond-M Connected outfit, no matter how good the brand blotting was."

"That's what stopped me from making any accusations. And Dad didn't want trouble with anyone else.

Besides he wasn't losing any more cows than were normal."

"A cowthief could run off Guthrie's stock, drive it over the county line and exchange it for other stock."

"That's possible. Dad heard a rumor once that Guthrie suspected Monroe, but after his cows were found with Rafter-F calves following them, that settled it. Dad was guilty in Guthrie's mind. There was more trouble too. Back in 1874 when barbed wire was beginning to be strung, Guthrie run a fence down the center of Horcado Creek, separating our holdings from his. It wasn't the same type wire you see nowadays, but vicious stuff that tore wounds in stock. Our horse and cows not realizing what it was, used to get into it and tear their hides. Then screw worm got into the wounds and completed the damage. Dad complained to Guthrie about it, which only made Guthrie mad, but eventually when some of his stock was being ruined, he removed the fence. And there were other little annoyances from time to time that didn't make for congenial friendships. Guthrie tried to buy Dad out on various occasions, but Dad refused to sell. Said he wasn't going to be 'bought out' of the country by anybody named Guthrie."

"But it was Monroe your father sold to—"

"And that deal never looked right to me. For all his cattle, Monroe was broke most of the time. He'd go away on trips and do a lot of gambling. And his luck didn't hold, according to him. Once he returned from one of his trips, married. I guess they didn't get along.

Anyway, she came to town to live. But that's none of my business. Dad and Monroe always got along okay, though Dad never trusted him overmuch. He decided he wanted a place where he could get off by himself, and he came up here and fixed up this place. Nick, the Tonkawa, came with him of course. Dad made it all legal with the state and bought all of Tourmaline. Then he fixed up this place to his liking. He never objected, though, if some prospector wanted to stay in one of these old houses."

"Did he think there'd ever be a good strike of tourmaline here?"

Fletcher shook his head. "No. I don't either. There was a miner up here about two months ago. He brought up dynamite and a lot of ideas where to hunt. All he ever did was blow a lot of holes in the earth. He left disgusted. Even left some of his dynamite and other stuff in the house where he was living. Maybe some day I'll find a use for it. I can't say I blame Dad for coming up here and leaving the outfit to be run by the foreman. I wasn't interested in raising beef and Dad knew it. He had all the money he wanted. I had a couple of years at a college in Nebraska, then came back. I still wanted to get away on my own. Dad gave me two hundred bucks and told me to get out and see the country and get the itch out of my hooves. So I saddled up and left. And I saw plenty of country. The money didn't last long after a couple of poker sessions. I'd take a job, work a month or so, and then. push on. I always gave Dad my new address and we'd exchange letters. I had a letter from Dad saying he had sold a bull to Webb Monroe. Monroe had claimed he wanted to improve his stock and that he liked Dad's breed. Anyway, Dad got his money and gave him a receipt and so on. Dad said that Monroe had wanted more stock but claimed he hadn't money for more and wanted Dad to take his note, but Dad didn't trust him that far. The next letter stated that Monroe wanted to buy the Rafter-F. Dad looked on that as a joke and told Monroe to produce twenty-thousand cash as a down payment and he'd listen to him, providing he furnished good security for the remaining thirty thousand."

Quist scowled. "One day, Monroe has only enough money to buy one bull and lacks the cash for more Rafter-F stock. Then, a short time later he tries to buy your Dad's ranch. Where could he get that much money so soon?"

"That's something I want to learn. I've got an idea, but no proof."

"What happened next?"

"Next—?" Fletcher swallowed hard and looked away. "Next I got a telegram from Sheriff Beadle telling me to come home at once, as Dad had been murdered by Indians—" He broke off, finding it difficult to continue. "Anyway, I returned home as soon as I could make it." His tone became harder. "When I heard Monroe claimed to have bought the Rafter-F for fifty-thousand cash, I felt certain something was wrong. And in view of Guthrie's enmity, I figured the two had ganged up in a crooked deal. Mort Beadle tried to persuade me otherwise, but I was beyond being reasoned with. Seeing Dad's mutilated body at the undertaker's did something to me, and I guess I lost my head—"

"And you started out to fill Monroe and Guthrie full of lead."

Fletcher frowned. "I'm not certain what I had in mind, Mr. Quist. I know a blind rage struck me, and I had my mind made up to get at the root of the matter, even if I had to shoot the truth out of those two. I spied the two sitting on the hotel gallery and started for them. Just as I was passing the Flying Hooves Livery, two men standing in the doorway undertook to stop me. The first shot missed. I managed a lucky shot and got one of them. The other bit me, but I dropped him too. As he fell his gun exploded and the wild shot hit and killed the sheriff's deputy. But by that time I had fainted from the shock. I was taken to the doctor's house. I hadn't been hit too bad but it laid me up for a time. I was still fighting mad and determined to have a showdown with Guthrie and Monroe. One night I escaped. By that time, of course, I was supposed to be under arrest. I got away, all right, but I'd overestimated my strength and I was captured within the week. So the next bed I got was in the jail cell, awaiting trial."

"Why arrest you? You'd been fired on first. You were only defending yourself—"

"Wait, Greg, you're hearing my story now. There

were others told a different story. One of the men who'd fired on me recovered, and swore he had seen me reaching for my gun to take a shot at Guthrie. That was a lie, but there were those who backed him up. However, there were more witnesses who swore I'd not even drawn my gun until I'd been fired on. That saved my neck, though the jury figured that I must have been looking for trouble and it refused to let me off scot-free. I drew a sentence for manslaughter and went to prison. Time off for good behavior got me out in ten months. I had a lot of time to think over things in prison, and I decided there was a chance, a very slim chance, I'd been wrong. Due to my actions, two men were dead, and a third wounded. I swore then I'd never carry a gun again, as long as I lived. It's probably just as well. Both the Guthrie and Monroe factions come to town, sometimes when I'm there. So long as I'm not wearing a gun, I can't be forced into any fights. And I don't go into Horcado City any more than I have to.

Quist said dryly, "Does any of that gang know how fast you can loose arrows?"

"I don't suppose so. I'm just an ex-con who makes archery equipment for a living, so far's they're concerned."

"I'll tell you one thing," Quist stated, "I'd hate to start an even draw with you."

"I'd not even release an arrow at a man, except in self-defense. I just don't like killing."

"Me either, but I've found it necessary—more times

than I like to think of. Scott, who were the two cowhands who fired on you that day?"

"As I got it, they were just a couple of saddle-tramps riding through who'd been hired by Guthrie that morning on Monroe's recommendation. There were those who figured them as a hired bodyguard."

"Looks that way to me," Quist frowned. "And why should Guthrie hire a bodyguard—if he did hire them—unless he expected trouble from you? I don't like it."

"No more do I, but what can I do? The one cowhand who lived got out of town before anyone had a chance to question him to any extent after the trial. While I was in prison I had my lawyer checking into the business of Monroe buying the Rafter-F. That also had to be cleared in the courts. Monroe's story was that he had paid Dad fifty-thousand cash. And he had a bill-of-sale, signed, with Dad's name. I can't deny that. I saw the bill. Monroe's story was that Dad said he had to go to Tourmaline but he'd meet Monroe in the Horcado bank the next day and they'd do up things, the deed and other papers, in more regular fashion. And I must admit Dad might have done something of the sort. If he'd planned to go to Tourmaline that day, he wouldn't have let anything interfere."

"All this was sworn to on oath in the court?" Quist asked.

Fletcher nodded. "Monroe went to the bank the next day. Dad didn't show up, of course. A rider was sent to the Rafter-F. The foreman said he'd not seen Dad since the previous day. The rider rode up to Tourmaline. Somebody had shot Dad and left a fresh-painted arrow stuck in his back. They blamed it on the Tonkawas. Though he had accompanied Dad to Tourmaline, the foreman said, Nick, the Tonkawa, was never seen again. So folks spoke of the treachery of Indians but I feel right sure that Nick must have been killed too. Anyway, the court, on the strength of the signed bill-of-sale, awarded the Rafter-F property to Webb Monroe. I was behind bars by that time and couldn't fight it. Anyway, my lawyer did all he could."

Quist swore softly under his breath. "It looks like to me that the court slipped. That bill-of-sale seems like mighty flimsy evidence, particularly with a man like Monroe—"

"There was the sheriff's signature as witness to the signing—"

"Mort Beadle?"

"Yeah, Mort Beadle. Everybody knew Mort and trusted him. He gave evidence in court, swore under oath that he had seen Monroe hand fifty-thousand dollars in cash and bills, to Dad, and he had also witnessed Dad's signature on the bill-of-sale. So what else could the court do but award the property to Monroe?"

"On that kind of evidence, I suppose so," Quist said slowly. "You don't suppose Beadle was hornswoggled in some way, do you?"

"I thought of that, but Mort's no fool. He was right friendly with me and admitted he hated to give evidence that would hurt me, but he had to tell the truth as he saw it.

"And the fifty thousand never was found?"

"Never. I've thought and thought—" Fletcher paused, then, "I've talked to everyone I knew might be some way involved, but I got no place. I'd had a rep as being wild when I left Horcado City, and by the time I was free again, I was just an ex-con. A lot of people I used to know didn't want to have anything to do with me. So I came up here—Dad's will left me all he had of course, which wasn't too much, cash-wise—and decided to start a new life for myself. I'm making out all right."

Quist said bluntly, "I think the whole business stinks. Either Beadle was fooled in some way, or he's a crook too."

"I'd hate to think that of Mort. He's one of the few friends I have left in town."

"Howcome Guthrie got the Rafter-F?"

"Monroe sold it to him for fifty-five thousand a month after the court awarded Monroe the deed."

"To me, it's as clear as the brand on a cow's hide. Your father refused to sell to Guthrie, so Guthrie furnished the money for Monroe to buy it. Then Monroe turned the property over to Guthrie—and I'll bet he made a good profit too."

"Yeah, I thought of that too," Fletcher said, "but where's the proof? Anyway, Monroe had the right to dispose of the property as he saw fit, and if Guthrie wanted to put through a deal like that, that's no crime either.

What gets me is Dad's signature to the bill-of-sale."

"How about forgery?"

"That's another thing I considered, and so did my lawyer. We got some of Dad's old checks and made comparisons. There were slight differences, but for that matter there were slight differences in the check signatures too. No one ever signs his name exactly the same when he writes it. There's always some minor change. Anyway, the court ruled it was Dad's signature, and with Mort Beadle's name as a witness, that was that."

"Damned if it satisfies me," Quist said bluntly. "I've got a hunch there's a weak link in the chain someplace, but I just can't put my finger on it. When I do, things will start to clear up. This business needs thought."

"Greg, where did you get that bow you brought with you? I noticed you carrying it the first day you were here. That's the reason I hailed you and asked if you were looking for me."

"I'll trade some information with you. Howcome you're friendly with Guthrie's daughter? I'm betting her father doesn't know it—"

X

"You're right there." Some color had crept into Fletcher's cheeks. "I knew Sheila as a kid, before I went away. Sheila was one of the few people who was decent to me when I had my trouble. Somehow we began to see more of each other. Guthrie heard about it and hit the ceiling, forbid her to see me. Fact is, he's not too keen on Sheila seeing any man near her own age. He's always running somebody off his doorstep—"

"Hates all suitors, eh?"

"That's about it. Though he does seem to be more in favor of Jeff Crawford, and doesn't grouch too much when Crawford calls on her. Anyway, Sheila continued to see me. I started to teach her how to shoot with a bow, we took rides and so on. Guthrie heard about it and got madder than ever. From then on, Sheila didn't tell him about it when she saw me. She rode up here one day, and later found Guthrie had put a rider on her trail. That made more of a rumpus. Guthrie threatened to send her out of the state to school. Things settled down after a time. I guess Guthrie thought he had her buffaloed. Now when I'm with her we try to avoid people. The first day you came up here, we thought you were somebody Guthrie had hired to watch her."

"So that's why you were so cordial," Quist smiled.

"Sometimes I wonder if I haven't forgotten how to be cordial," Fletcher said moodily. "Neither of us like this sort of hiding out from folks. I put up with it solely on Sheila's account. She's getting mighty tired of it too. I suppose you saw how things stand with us."

Quist said dryly, "What I couldn't see, I could imagine."

"You can see my position, Greg. I can't go to Guthrie, even if he'd listen to sense. He hates me now instead of my Dad. But you know all that. What about that bow you brought with you? Where did you get it?"

Quist told him of finding the skeleton and the bow. Fletcher's eyes widened as he listened to the story; he grinned widely when Quist told of leaving the two pine slats wrapped in newspaper. "I just figured," Quist concluded, "with so many people trying to get that bow, somebody might get the idea of stealing it when I was away from the hotel room. What do you make of it?"

"I'm wondering if that Indian skeleton could be all that is left of Nick, the Tonkawa. I'd like to see it."

"I can take you to the place. What do you make of that bow, Scott?"

"My father made that bow."

"You're certain."

"In the first place he favored osage for bows. Second, I know he made an extra fine bow for Nick— and that bow was a good one when new. Third, Dad always stamped his initials in the bows he made, with a pair of very small dies."

"I didn't see any initials."

"I'll show you." Fletcher rose from the table where they sat, got the old bow from the bench and returned. "You didn't see the initials, Greg, because you weren't expecting anything of the sort. The wood is dirty and weathered. They've almost disappeared. I knew where to look for them. Look here, near the handle, on the belly—the rounded side." With one fingernail, Fletcher scraped away a bit of sediment from the weathered osage. Quist took the bow and in the light from the lamp, barely managed to discern the two initials B.F., in tiny letters.

"You're right," he nodded. He examined the bow further, gripping it by the handle. "This isn't much like the bow I had when I was a kid. They make them longer nowdays. Another thing, the bow I had was flat, with the handle just sort of rounded. This handle is built up, so it really fits a man's hand."

"Yes, it affords a better grip. There's a riser used to build it up. I remember Dad saying one time that Nick had unusually large hands for a man his size, so I suppose he built this to Nick's size. I'll say one thing, that rawhide doesn't look as neat as Dad used to wind them. I suppose the weather has tightened it and loosened it and tightened it again from time to time. Probably birds and animals fretted it some too." He laughed shortly. "I'm already taking it for granted this is the bow Nick had."

"I'm beginning to think so myself. What say we ride up there and look at that skeleton tomorrow morning?"

"Suits me," Fletcher said. "And you'd better figure to sleep here tonight. Unless you have to get back to town."

"I'm agreeable to stay, Scott." Then, as Scott rose to put the bow back on the bench. "Put that bow someplace where no one can find it easily."

Fletcher paused. "Any particular reason?"

Quist scowled. "Hunch, that's all. If somebody wants that bow so bad, I want it handy too. I wouldn't want anybody just coming in here and picking it up sometime when you're away."

"Maybe you've got a good idea." He considered a few moments, then said, "Let me have that table a minute." The table was cleared and Quist wondered what he had in mind when he dragged the table to the center of the room, placed a chair upon it and then mounted to the chair. "Now if you'll hand me that piece of tarpaulin on the bench," Fletcher said.

By the time Quist had secured the section of tarpaulin, and glanced up, he saw .a square opening in the roof. "Cripes! You've got a trapdoor in your ceiling. I hadn't noticed that."

Fletcher nodded, wrapping the old bow in the tarpaulin. "Yes, Dad put it in. Right slick job too, fits flush with the boards and unless you were looking for something of the sort, you'd never notice it. Dad was right handy with tools that way. He often said he wished he'd become a cabinet maker." Fletcher shoved the tarpaulin-wrapped bow out on the roof, replaced the trap door and got down from the table. "Dad used to say the opening made a good draft through here on the hot days. Well, I guess that bow will be safe on the roof, until we need it."

The table and chair were moved back to their former positions. The men talked a while longer, then extinguished the lamp and got into the bunks. It was long before Quist was able to sleep. Embers from the fireplace threw jumping lights about the room and he lay watching them while his mind turned over the various possibilities relative to Fletcher's problems. One thing was certain, there was something damnably wrong about the deal Monroe had made for the Rafter-F property, despite Mort Beadle's signature as witness on the paper.

XI

Quist strolled casually the length of Tourmaline's bedraggled street, stopping only when it dropped abruptly off to the more even terrain far below. By shading his eyes against the almost level rays of the brilliant sun, he could make out the rooves of Horcado City and the shining rails of the T.N. & A.S. where they ran far from the distant east past the town and then curved to swing around the great granite shoulder jutting from the mountains on which Tourmaline was situated.

He put out his cigarette and was about to turn back when he thought he saw riders raising dust on the trail from town. He watched for a moment more until they had disappeared behind a clump of mesquite, then, the sun bright in his eyes, he headed back for Fletcher's place. Fletcher was already busy with a frying pan before the fireplace.

"This clear air and the smell of that coffee," Quist laughed, "makes me so damned hungry, I'm ready to eat anything that doesn't bite me first."

"I got some ham when I was in town yesterday. And hen-fruit. It'll be on in a jiffy. Coffee's ready and if you'll throw a few knifes and forks on the table, we'll get at it."

They were nearly through breakfast when Quist, said, "I think I saw some horses heading up this way."

Fletcher looked up quickly. "You're sure?"

"Not certain no. It just looked like they were heading along your trail. Three of 'em."

"Probably Bench-G hands looking for strays."

"By the dust they were raising they weren't looking very close."

"Well, if they come up here, we'll know it. Maybe we'd better not leave at once. Might as well wash up the dishes while we're waiting."

They lingered over coffee and cigarettes, then cleaned up the dishes. Quist said once, "It's damn nice up here, Scott. I envy you."

They went to the corral and saddled their horses, then led the animals back to the house. Quist suggested going down to the end of the street and taking another look for the riders. "Wouldn't do any good, by this time," Fletcher said. "You don't get so good a view in that direction."

They waited a while longer then rose to their feet as they heard the sounds of hoofs striking rocky soil. A few minutes later, Deputy Jeff Crawford rode into view, greeted them and dismounted, his pony's reins trailing.

"Well, this is a relief," Crawford chuckled.

The other two greeted him and Quist said, "What's a relief, Jeff?"

"Finding you here, Greg. We didn't know what had happened."

"Happened in what way?" Quist frowned.

"Well, you weren't at your hotel last night. I checked several times and you hadn't returned. Mort got worried—"

"Why should he?"

"Well, we didn't know—you see—well, after your trouble with Vink Fisher. And you'd had words with Brose Daulton too. Anyway, Mort got to thinking you'd had a ruckus with one or the other, or maybe both. Only other thing that could have happened, Mort figured, was that you might be up here."

"Damned considerate of you," Quist laughed. "Didn't realize folks worried over a railroad dick to that extent. You must have got a mighty early start."

Crawford gathered his reins, then swung the horse around. "Greg, I suppose you'll be back in town by tonight, eh?"

"So far's I know now," Quist replied.

"I'll see you then." Crawford touched spurs to his pony and rode off, to disappear beyond the gnarled live oak trees.

When he had gone, Quist and Fletcher exchanged glances. Fletcher said, "So now you're in Sheila's class. You've got someone riding herd on you." He was grinning widely.

Quist nodded. "Somebody's getting damn good and

worried, Scott. They're wondering what I'm up to, and following my movements as much as possible. And when folks get worried, they often make mistakes. And I'm waiting for someone to make just one bad move."

"You figuring Crawford is one of those folks?"

"Or Beadle. Or—hell, I don't know what to think yet. Let's get started."

"Be with you in a minute." Fletcher entered the house and emerged a few minutes later carrying one of his hunting bows. A doeskin quiver of arrows rattled at his back, their elongated triangular feathers shining silkily in the bright morning sunshine. He wasn't wearing a coat; a leather armguard protected his left forearm.

Quist swung up to his saddle. "You figuring to do some shooting, Scott?"

"I've got broadheads in my quiver. We might stir up some game. Anyway, it's more or less a habit to take archery tackle when I go away from the house. Never know what you'll see." He climbed aboard his horse and they started.

Quist was able to give the general direction and Fletcher pointed out a couple of shortcuts they could take as the riders passed through mountain juniper and between great granite blocks. At times the horses' hooves slipped on loose chunks of granite, as they carried the men down grades and up steep passes. Eventually, Quist once more took over the lead. After a time he spoke, "If I'm not mistaken,

Scott, that skeleton's just beyond that massive rock yonderly—see, the one rounded at the top with a sort of pinkish color running through the gray—big as your house, it looks. It was in shadow when I found it. The way the sun is, the shadow will be still deeper now."

Five minutes later they had dismounted, the skeleton's bones almost at their feet. Quist glanced quickly over the earth; things looked pretty much as he had left them. There were no fresh footprints since his own had been made. He said, "What do you make of it?"

"Not much," Fletcher frowned. "Those ribs look as though they'd encountered some lead."

"Somebody sure perforated him, all right." Quist mentioned the three bullets and red glass beads he'd found when he'd sifted the coarse gritty sand. "For all I know there might have been more slugs."

Fletcher picked up the withered moccasins, dropped them again. He appeared to be searching for something. He ranged wider around the body, pushed aside a stunted mesquite bush and peered back of it. "Damn funny," he muttered. Quist asked what was funny. Fletcher explained, "If this was once Nick, the Tonkawa, where's his quiver? Bow's no good to a man without a quiver of arrows."

"I thought of that too. Maybe he was forced to leave someplace in a hurry, and didn't have time to get his quiver. Or someone else may have found it here and taken it."

"In that case, why not take the bow too? For that matter, Greg, why did you take the bow?"

"I'm damned if I know. Just following some sort of hunch, I reckon. And that hunch has apparently stirred up a hornet's nest." Quist frowned. "Let's suppose he had to leave your father's place in a hurry. The quiver might have been left there. Maybe he saw the murderer, or murderers, coming and lit out fast as he could."

Fletcher shrugged. "Could be." He stopped and picked up the withered leather sack with its dangling rawhide thongs. One of the thongs had a knot in it. A few tiny glass beads still clung to the edge of the small sack. "This could be Nick's old medicine bag," he commented. "I seem to remember seeing it, and it had beads like these sewn to the edge. Lord knows what he carried in it to ward off bad spirits. More beads, maybe, and a few strands of some enemy's hair. I remember he had a set of rattles from a diamondback, he set great store by—God only knows why."

"Probably felt about it like some people do carrying a rabbit's foot," Quist said. "Could be it was the first rattler he ever killed, and he felt strong carrying the rattles in that little bag around his neck."

"Maybe." Fletcher seemed lost in thought. "I do remember Dad telling Nick one time that he'd make him such a good bow he wouldn't need his medicine bag any more. Just the same, I never remember seeing Nick without the bag, though I didn't see too much of him."

"Whatever was in it, is gone now," Quist observed. "I'm just wondering about whoever shot him, were they looking in the bag for something?"

"What makes you think that?"

Quist took the medicine sack from Fletcher's hand and indicated the two dangling rawhide thongs. "One of those thongs has been cut, is my guess. You can see the knot still in the other one. Somebody didn't bother to take time loosening the knot. Therefore, somebody emptied the bag looking for—what? I wish to hell I could figure it out."

"Maybe he had something of Dad's—or maybe somebody thought he had. But why murder him in the first place? Nick was a pretty decent sort of cuss; he left his own people to follow Dad—"

"And if I'm not mistaken," Quist frowned, "that's what brought about his death but I can't figure why. Well, seen enough?"

Fletcher nodded. "I can't think of any reason for staying around here any longer. I can't be sure of course, but if that skeleton isn't Nick's, then I'm 'way wide of the mark."

They scooped sand over the old dried bones, then went to their horses, mounted and started the return journey.

They were two thirds of the way back when it happened:

With Fletcher riding on his left, they were crossing a fairly level stretch, with a great outcropping of granite wall. To the right, the terrain rose slightly and was strewn with a tumble of huge boulders. The horses were moving scarcely faster than a walk.

Quist heard something spat-flatten against the rock to Fletcher's left, turned his head to see the silvery glint of a mashed bullet just as the sound of the shot reached his ear. He was already leaving the saddle when he heard the second shot.

XII

"You okay, Scott?" Quist snapped quickly.

"Okay. You?"

"They're rotten shots," Quist spat.

Both were keeping low. "Who do you suppose it is?" Fletcher asked.

"Somebody that doesn't want me nosing around any longer," Quist said grimly.

Fletcher said coolly, "Don't be hoggish. I think one of those shots were meant for me."

"You're welcome to both of 'em," Quist grunted. Cautiously he raised his head and surveyed the gradual rocky slope. There wasn't a soul to be seen.

Abruptly, Quist felt the sombrero jerk on his head. The shot echoed through. the hills as Quist again ducked down. "Better shots than I thought," he snapped, immediately peering above his shelter again. The bullet had brushed the edge of his sombrero.

Some two hundred feet distant he saw black powder-smoke rising above the rocks. Now he had one of the would-be assassins spotted. He dropped abruptly as a leaden slug whined past his ear.

"Persistent bastards, aren't they?" he growled.

"You'd best stay down, Greg," Fletcher said anxiously.

"Hell, they could keep us pinned here all day."

"All right, let's rush 'em then," Fletcher proposed.

"And you with no gun?"

"I'll make out."

"Wait a sec. I've got a better idea."

He rose cautiously and cast a quick glance in the direction in which he'd seen the black powdersmoke. Directly back of the spot was a wide slab of uptilted granite. Quist felt the forty-four jerk in his fist as be released a slug from his gunmuzzle.

There came a startled yell of "Jesus!" and a man leaped frantically into view. Instantly Quist fired a second shot. The man stumbled, the rifle flying from his grasp and he went sprawling to the rocks.

"C'mon!" Quist bawled. "Now we rush the other hombre from two sides!"

The ruse worked. Farther up the slope, a man leaped into view and went scrambling frantically, in full retreat, farther up the grade, dodging this way and that.

Twang! . . . *Twang!* Quist turned in time to see two arrows in flight. Even as he saw the fleeing man's hat fly into the air, the fellow stumbled and went sprawling, a broadhead through his thigh.

"Looks to me like you don't need a gun," Quist

snapped. "C'mon, let's see what we've bagged."

"But, Greg, I don't see how you forced that first scut into the open." They were picking their way across the broken clutter of rocks.

"Fired my first shot at the slab of granite at his back, figuring it might ricochet close enough to scare him into the open. And it did." They went on. "Looked to me like you did a good job yourself, Scott. Hold up a bit, let me go first."

Gun in hand, Quist approached the first man who sat on the ground, eyes wide with fear. "Don't kill me—" he started.

"Shut up, you scut!" Quist snapped. He reached down and jerked the six-shooter from the man's holster and tossed it to one side. The fellow's rifle lay some distance off.

"Get me a doctor, fellers. I'm dying."

"Looks like a shoulder wound to me. Hell, you're not hurt bad," Fletcher said. The man closed his eyes and slumped sidewise.

Quist said disgustedly, "Fainted, by God. Know him, Scott?"

Fletcher nodded. "Name's Frank Tilford. One of Monroe's crew."

"Let's go look at the other hombre. This one will stay where he is for a spell."

They scrambled over loose rock until they reached the other wounded man. He greeted them defiantly with a string of curses. "Get this goddam arrow out of my laig. I want a doctor."

"What you want and what you're going to get are two different things," Quist threatened, "if you don't shut your dirty mouth."

He was still clutching the forty-four in his hand and glanced meaningly at it.

Something of fear crept into the fellow's eyes, and he glanced away, begging Fletcher to "get this damn arrow outten me, Fletcher."

Quist reached down and disposed of the Colt gun at the man's side. His rifle too lay a few yards off. Fletcher drew his knife and bent over the man. The sharp steel broad-head had gone through the thigh up to the feathers. With his blade, Fletcher cut the head from the birch arrow and dropped the sharp steel head into his quiver. Then he withdrew the arrow from the other end and tossed it to one side. Blood poured copiously from the wound. The leg of the man's trousers was cut open and with the fellow's bandanna and one of his own, Fletcher bandaged it as tight as he could.

"Know him?" Quist asked.

"Bert Sheldon. Works for Guthrie's Bench-G."

Sheldon's face was ashen now; beads of sweat stood on his forehead. Quist said, "Who put you up to this, Sheldon?"

"Nobody. It—it was all a mistake."

"You made a mistake all right," Quist growled. "Where's your horses?"

The man stammered out directions to the mounts' hiding place.

"I'll go get them," Fletcher offered. He left, picked

up Sheldon's sombrero on his way, and removed the arrow from the crown of the felt. Then he went picking his way carefully through the rocks.

Quist looked down at Sheldon. "Anything you want to tell me, now, may make it easier for you later, Sheldon."

"Oh, Christ, get me to a doctor before I bleed to death," Sheldon groaned. "I ain't sayin' nothing until then."

Quist left him and went back to look at Tilford. Tilford was conscious again. Quist questioned him. Tilford said, between moans, that he had mistaken Quist and Fletcher for somebody else that he and Sheldon had had trouble with.

"You're lying," Quist snapped.

Tilford swore he was telling the truth. He too started begging for medical attention.

"You'll get a doctor when we hit Horcado City and not before," Quist said wrathfully. He saw Fletcher coming, leading two horses behind him and went to meet him.

"I think we should get Sheldon and Tilford to town soon's possible," Fletcher said. "We can stop at my place and I'll do what I can, and then we'd better push on."

Quist nodded. "But if I did what I felt like doing, I'd keep these two scuts here and make 'em talk. Only I lack the guts to do it."

"I know how you feel." Fletcher examined Sheldon's bandage, loosened it a moment and again rebandaged. Together they got the wounded man on his horse and lashed him into place with his lariat. A few minutes later, Tilford was fixed up in the same manner. It took but a few minutes more to get the other horses, then they started back, Quist and Fletcher each leading a horse carrying a wounded man.

"Your bull's-eye must have jumped off your range," Quist said a little later. "I saw Sheldon's hat go sailing off his head, and then your next arrow found pay-dirt."

"That first shot was a mite closer than I intended," Fletcher confessed. "'r misjudged the wind some, where it came over that rise."

"And lowered your sights plenty on the second shot?"

"His back made a broader target," Fletcher said meaningly. Quist looked steadily at him a moment, remembering what Fletcher had said about not liking killing. Fletcher said defensively, "You needn't look at me like that, Greg. Jeepers! You plugged Tilford in the shoulder."

"All right," Quist grouched. "I could tell you I was just acting humane, but I won't. Hell-bells! I was just shooting to stop the scut that had been trying to finish me any way I knew how. Tilford's just lucky. And you know damn well you can't make a man talk when he's dead."

Fletcher laughed. "Just about as I figured."

It was nearly three in the afternoon before they

pulled rein in front of Fletcher's place in Tourmaline. Both Sheldon and Tilford looked all in, but both were conscious. They wouldn't say anything beyond asking to be given medical attention. Both men were unlashed from their saddles and assisted to chairs inside the house.

Fletcher said suddenly, "Judas Priest! Somebody's been nosing around here while we were gone. Look, Greg, those bunks were made before we left. Look at the blankets—all rumpled. And several of my bows have been taken down and not replaced."

"Anything missing?" Quist asked.

"Not that I notice right now." He and Quist both glanced toward the ceiling, but the trapdoor hadn't been moved apparently. "Guess there's no harm done." He went to a small cabinet in one corner and returned with strips of cloth rolled into bandages, a hypodermic syringe, and some bottles containing drugs.

Quist looked curiously at him. "All prepared aren't you?"

"Prepared, yes, but this is the first time I've ever had any use for this stuff since I came to live here—aside from a few minor cuts I picked up from time to time. I worked in the hospital for a spell when I was in the—when I was living at state expense. Get me some water, will you, Greg?"

Sheldon and Tilford were doctored while they sat in chairs. Sheldon was cared for first, and he sat stoically through Fletcher's ministerings. The arrow wound was swabbed medically, then rebandaged with only a few groans and gritting of teeth from the man. Tilford, on the other hand, yelped like a stuck pig when his turn came.

"Quit your whining," Fletcher said disgustedly, "you're not being hurt that bad. The slug is lodged in the fleshy part of your shoulder, just alongside the armpit. Cripes, I can feel it under the skin. I can get it out in a jiffy, if you'll just hold still, and the sooner it comes out, the better for you, Tilford—" Fletcher was working as he talked. A sharp blade gleamed momentarily, the bleeding increased. Tilford drew a long shuddering groan.

Fletcher worked steadily for several minutes. "Damn it, I can feel the end of that slug, but it acts like its glued in there. Greg, hold this to the wound for a minute—" handing Quist a chunk of bandaging. He left his patient and went to one of the workbenches where Quist could hear him muttering in frustrated tones.

Quist said, "What's wrong?"

"I had a pair of needlenosed pliers right here and now I can't find them. Certainly whoever was messing around here while we were gone wouldn't take a pair of pliers." He searched a few moments more, then said, "Lucky, I've got another pair."

He rummaged around beneath the bench, jerked out a box of various tools and searched through that. Then he returned, bearing a pair of small pliers with long thin jaws. Seizing a bottle of alcohol, he poured it generously over the pliers, then again went to work. There came a sharp yelp from Tilford, and the sound of a small chunk of lead being dropped to the floor. Followed more swabbing and bandaging.

"And these two had best be got to the doctor as soon as possible," Fletcher said, washing his hands.

"They're headed for the sheriff's office," Quist said hard-voiced. "He can get the doctor if he likes. These murderin' scuts have already got more attention than they deserve. Let's get 'em on horses, and I'll start."

"I'm going with you, Greg."

"Maybe it would be best if you didn't, Scott." He and Fletcher exchanged glances. "No use stirring up any trouble for yourself. Besides you got a bloody floor to mop up before it stains."

The two men were once more lashed into saddles, no fight at all in them now. Quist climbed into his saddle and Fletcher handed him the reins of both other horses. "You sure you can make it all right, Greg?"

"I won't have any trouble."

"Better loosen that bandage of Sheldon's for a few minutes, every so often on the way."

"I'll take care of it," Quist nodded, and departed, leading the two horses at his rear. . . .

He had nearly reached town when he heard loping hoofs at his rear. Turning in the saddle, he recognized Mead Guthrie approaching. Guthrie slowed gait as he reached Quist's side, casting sidelong glances at the two wounded captives.

"You, eh, Quist?" Guthrie's tones boomed in the evening silence. "What's up? You taking these two captive—Hey"—after a closer look—"That's Bert Sheldon you got there. What in hell does this mean?"

"It means they got their asses in a trap," Quist said shortly. "They're on their way to jail—"

"But, look here, Quist, Sheldon is one of my men. You can't do this—"

"I'm doing it," Quist snapped. "And don't try to stop me, Guthrie—"

"Now don't you go getting proddy with me, Quist," Guthrie growled. "I want to know what this is all about."

Quist said wearily, "These two hombres got reckless with their Winchesters and they had to be stopped."

"You—you mean they fired on you?" Guthrie's jaw dropped.

"That's the way it looked. Maybe they were just trying to see how close they could come without hitting me. Maybe it was a game and they had bets on it."

"But why should they fire on you?"

"Maybe you can answer that better than I can," Quist said coldly.

"Me? What in hell would I know about it?"

"That's what I intend to find out. Howcome you happened along just at this time?"

"It's none of your gawddam business, Quist, but I'd just as soon tell you. I sent Sheldon in to pick up my mail early this mornin'. When he didn't show up I come in to find out why—"

"How many more of your hands were supposed to be in town this morning?" Quist cut in.

"Just Sheldon. All the rest of my crew are out to the ranch, earning their wages. You must think I'm another Monroe to let my hands hang around town all the time. By Gawd, there's something funny about this." He dropped back, next to Sheldon. "Bert, I want to know what this is all about. You been throwing lead at Quist?"

Sheldon raised his white face for a moment. "You heard Quist, Guthrie. Did you think he was putting conumdrums to you?" His head dropped again.

"Gawddamit, Sheldon, I don't want none of your insolence! What's back of this? Where's the mail you were sent to pick up?"

"At the post office s'far's I know. Now go 'way, Guthrie, I don't feel like talkin'."

"If I yank you out of that saddle—" Gurthrie started hotly.

"You'll do nothing of the sort," Quist snapped. "If you're so damn' eager to be doing something, keep a civil tongue in your head and ride ahead to town. Tell Mort Beadle he'll be needing a doctor for two prisoners shortly."

"Look here, Quist, you aren't giving me orders—"

"It was a suggestion, not an order," Quist said evenly. "All I ask is for you to keep out of my way. Now suit yourself."

Guthrie fumed, but didn't reply for a moment. When he did, his voice shook with anger. "By Gawd, I aim to get at the bottom of this. We'll see what the sheriff has to say about you going around plugging anybody you feel like."

He kicked his horse in the ribs and spurred furiously toward town.

Quist looked after him, wondering, "Now who's the liar? Jeff Crawford said he was riding with two Bench-G hands this morning. Guthrie denies that anyone but Sheldon went to town."

From behind in a croaking voice came Sheldon's tones, "Thanks for taking that big blowhard down a mite, Quist. He's had it coming."

"No thanks necessary, Sheldon. Unless you feel like telling me who hired you to ambush us—"

"Don't tell him nothin'," came a shriek from Frank Tilford. "We ain't done nothin' wrong. It was all a mistake—"

"Aw, shut up," Sheldon said disgustedly. "I'm not tellin' anythin', 'cause there's nothing to tell. Like you say, Frank, it was all a big mistake."

XIII

Lights gleamed along Trail Street when Quist led his two captives into Horcado City. There weren't too many people on the street, but someone took note of the two men tied in their saddles and within a short time a number of men were trailing along behind, asking questions which Quist ignored.

A doctor was waiting when Quist reached the sheriff's office—Doctor Luke Nash, a spare man past middle-age in rumpled gray clothing. There was no sign of Mead Guthrie when Quist and his two prisoners halted at the hitchrack. Beadle, the doctor and Jeff Crawford had been waiting on the porch and now hurried out across the sidewalk.

The sheriff asked, "What in God's name happened, Quist? Mead Guthrie said you—"

"Where's Guthrie now?"

"He was in such a state, demanding your arrest and so on, I told him to go cool off."

"I'm surprised he took orders that way. Or maybe he didn't want to stay and be questioned."

"Questioned about what? What happened—"

Crawford cut in, "That's Bert Sheldon and Frank Tilford—"

The doctor interrupted, "I'm Doctor Nash, Mr. Quist. Perhaps you'd better let me examine those men as soon as possible."

"I won't keep you," Quist said. "They've both already had some attention from Scott Fletcher and he did a pretty good job looks like."

"Scott Fletcher? Is he in on this business?" Beadle snapped.

Quist told it briefly: "Scott and I were up looking at that Indian skeleton. On our way back, Sheldon and Tilford tried to dry-gulch us. It was a mistake on their part—as they've already admitted."

The sheriff scowled. "Fletcher's started toting a gun again, eh? He's kept out of trouble as long as he could and now he's cut loose again—"

"I didn't say he was toting a gun," Quist said sharply, "and don't be so ready to find fault with Scott, sheriff. Any blame you start pushing around, can be pushed on me—"

"I don't like your manner, Quist," Beadle bridled. "I could put you under arrest, you know."

"Don't try it. I'd be bailed out so fast it would make your head swim. And. then I'd really go after you, Beadle."

Beadle said sullenly, "There's nothing to prevent me from arresting Fletcher, anyway."

"On what charge?" Quist demanded. "I dare you to try it."

Jeff Crawford said, "Take it easy, Mort. We haven't got the story yet. Maybe it wasn't Quist's fault."

"I've told the story," Quist stated harshly. "And just the minute Doctor Nash says these men are able to be questioned, there'll be more of the story brought out. You may not like what you're going to hear, sheriff."

Wheeling his horse away from the tierail, Quist headed in the direction of the T.N. & A.S. station.

Arriving at the railroad depot he dismounted and learned at the grilled window that a telegram awaited him. He accepted it, read the words through in silence, then stuck it in his pocket. Getting a telegraph blank from the agent he sent a message to Jay Fletcher, Superintendent of Divisions:

TWO GUNS ARE ALWAYS BETTER THAN ONE AND THE EXTRA AUTHORITY MIGHT COME HANDY .   QUIST.

The stationmaster checked the words. "Come away without an extra gun, Mr. Quist? I've got one at home I could let you have."

"No, thanks. You might say that's a code message. Jay will know what's wanted."

"I hope you're not expecting any trouble in Horcado City."

"Trouble?" Quist looked surprised. "In a peaceful little town like this?"

Leaving a rather puzzled station man, Quist left the station and remounted. He left his horse at the livery stable, crossed diagonally to the hotel and mounted the steps to his room, after getting his key at the desk.

He opened his door cautiously, listened intently a moment before entering. Then he went in, closed the door behind him and lighted the lamp. He looked quickly to tht spot where he had left the two strips of pine, packaged in newspaper, on the floor against the wall. The package was no longer there.

Quist laughed softly. "Somebody's sure going to be disappointed when they find what's rolled in those newspapers."

He lowered the shades then proceeded to shave and change his shirt. He dusted his clothing and boots, re-donned his underarm harness and coat, slipped the sombrero on his head and once more descended the stairs. In the lobby, the elderly clerk was engaged in conversation with a tall man of middle-age in citizen's clothing, with pleasant features. Quist paused a moment at the desk and was introduced to Merle Inwood, proprietor of the hotel. "I hope you find yourself comfortable, Mr. Quist," Inwood said when they had shaken hands.

"I was wondering," Quist said, "if the keys to the doors fit all rooms, or if they're different?"

"Certainly not, Mr. Quist. Each door lock has its own key." He sounded a trifle indignant. "Can't you see—?" He broke off. "Is anything wrong?"

"I left a package in my room yesterday and now it's missing."

Both Inwood and the clerk looked aghast. "You're sure you're not mistaken, Mr. Quist?" Inwood asked.

"I'm not mistaken."

Inwood looked quickly at the clerk. The clerk said, "Mr. Quist's key was on its hook when I came on duty. I noticed it there yesterday, too. When you didn't come in last night, Mr. Quist, I looked to see if you were in your room, but your key was on its hook. So nobody's had your key."

"No chance of somebody getting the key when you were away from the desk?" Quist asked.

"I leave the desk for only very short times and not often. The day clerk does the same. Generally we try to see that somebody's here if we have to leave for a moment."

Inwood looked worried. "And I'd swear to the honesty of the woman who cleans your room and makes your bed, Mr. Quist. She's been with me a long time. And she's the only one of the help who would have occasion to go upstairs during the day." He paused. "I hope nothing valuable is missing."

"Not at all," Quist laughed. "Matter of fact, it was your property that was taken." He furnished an explanation. "Yesterday one of the lower drawers in the dresser stuck and I yanked on it too hard. Two strips of wood split from the back when I pulled it out. They were rather splintery so I wrapped them in newspaper so no body'd get stuck and intended to bring them down and tell you to put the damage on my bill—"

"No, sir, Mr. Quist, we won't do that," Inwood said. "I'm just relieved that nothing valuable was taken. It's possible of course that the woman who cleans noticed the drawer was broken and found the slats. I'll inquire when she comes on duty in the morning. Just the same she shouldn't pick up packages that way. I'll speak to her about it."

The men talked a few minutes more, then Quist left to eat dinner. One glance showed him the dining room was full and no tables available, so he turned back and headed for the bar. Keg Hooper was talking to a man in cow-puncher togs when Quist entered. There were no others there at the time. Keg slid a bottle of beer and glass on the bar and said, "Meet Cody Hayden, Mr. Quist. Cody runs the Rocking-H spread."

Quist shook hands with Hayden, a tall well-built man with dark eyes and a trim mustache. He looked to be nearing forty, and was the type some women consider handsome. A large cameo ring decorated one finger on his left hand; his black string tie and white shirt were spotless, his boots shined. He'd been nursing a drink of whisky when Quist entered.

"Maybe I can get the news from the source, now, Mr. Quist," he smiled.

"What news is that?" Quist asked, sampling his glass of brew.

Hayden explained. "I was down to the War-Drum Saloon a spell back and Mead Guthrie was growling about you running rough-shod over folks—and Mead's the last one to make that accusation—and that Mort Beadle was just as bad. Guthrie claims you plugged one of his men this afternoon and he can't find out what it's about. And the sheriff told him just as good as to go on about his business and wouldn't tell him either."

"I'm not sure what it's all about myself yet," Quist replied. "Scott Fletcher and I were riding up in the mountains today and a couple of hombres tried to dry-gulch us—damned if I know why. We outfoxed 'em and convinced them of their mistake."

"Scott Fletcher toting his gun again?" Hayden asked. Quist shook his head. "He don't need a gun when he's got his bow, Hayden."

Hayden's eyes widened. "You mean he actually shot a man with a bow and arrow. I didn't think—would you believe it? With a bow and arrow!"

"It was just the arrow that did the damage," Quist said dryly. "And I had some luck with a shot."

Hayden asked more questions and Quist gave brief details. "So that's what happened;" Hayden said. "I don't know why Beadle had to be so damn secretive about it. I asked him about it and he just sort of told me to mind my own business—words to that effect. You'd think I wasn't a taxpayer, and him in my employ. Damn him, he's getting awful nasty the last few days. I never get a civil word from him any more. Someday, Mort Beadle and I are going to have a showdown. He's been in office too long."

Hayden poured another drink down his throat, said "so-long" and departed from the barroom. Quist chuckled, "Sounded as though Mort Beadle might have hurt Hayden's feelings."

"Hell, those two have been niffnawing for a couple of years."

"What about?"

"Leila Monroe."

"T'hell you say."

"I guess that started it anyway," Keg went on, swabbing the bar with a damp towel. "After she got her divorce from Monroe, about half the town begin to get ideas. Four or more years back, it looked to be settled that she'd marry Mort. Next thing I knew Cody Hayden and Mead Guthrie were buzzing around—"

"Not Guthrie!"

"I'm telling you, Mr. Quist. Why not? Mead considers himself quite a man, his wife is dead. It got so he and the sheriff weren't too friendly for a time, but I guess Mead got over it. Then one time there was a song and dance troupe came to town, to play the opry house. The sheriff had figured to take Mrs. Monroe, but somehow she switched to Cody Hayden. The next day Cody and Mort had words. Nobody knew what it was about for sure, but everybody made a guess. They got to calling names and Mort knocked Cody down. Jeff Crawford stepped in before Cody could pull his gun and stopped things, but Cody swore that some day he'd get Mort. But that too blew over, and the sheriff and Cody pretended to be friendly."

"Looks like Mrs. Monroe is playing the field. Who's got the inner track at present?"

"Well, it looked for a time like Merle Inwood, when she went to work at the hotel. But Jeff Crawford hangs around a lot too. Some of his time though he goes out to call on Guthrie's daughter."

"I figure he might be wasting his time."

"What do you know about it."

"Ask me no questions and I'll tell you no lies," Quist smiled.

"Looks like you favor Scott."

"I like him. Particularly after seeing him in action today."

"What actually happened, Mr. Quist?"

"Just what you heard me tell Hayden. And I've no idea why two men from Guthrie's and Monroe's outfits should take potshots at us. Well, I guess I'll go see if the dining room is cleared out a little."

"Watch your step"—as Quist started to leave.

Quist paused at the doorway to the lobby. "What do you mean by that?"

Keg Hooper grinned widely. "Nothing much, except

Mrs. Monroe was heard to tell the day clerk that one Gregory Quist looked to be pretty much of a man."

Quist flushed. "You go to hell, Keg," he said genially, and passed on through the lobby into the dining room.

Most of the diners had left by this time. Leila Monroe was nowhere in sight when he entered, so he found a table in one far corner. A Mexican girl in a white apron took his order. A few minutes later, Mrs. Monroe came in, nodded to Quist and went to consult with one of the remaining diners. He could hear her low laughter across the room, and his eyes followed her when she went to another table, her walk graceful, easy. Tonight she was dressed in a becoming gray.

Quist's eyes followed her movements about the room. He found himself wishing she'd come to his table, and then mentally chided himself. What you aiming to do, Greg? he asked himself. Start bucking all that competition? Let's see—Guthrie, Mort Beadle, Inwood, Cody Hayden, Jeff Crawford, and Lord knows how many others. The queen bee and her hive. Well, I can't say I blame a one of 'em. After all, in a cowtown like this, there aren't too many eligible women with her looks and get-up.

The Mexican girl had brought him his second cup of coffee and he'd finished his pie by the time the dining room emptied. He was rolling a cigarette and lighting it when he saw Leila Monroe approaching, bearing a cup in one hand. Quist exhaled and rose from his chair.

"May I hope I'm going to have company?"

"If you don't mind, Mr. Quist. I just had to sit down for a few minutes and I needed some coffee."

He pulled out a chair for her and she sat down. "I'm deeply honored," he said.

She wrinkled her nose at him. "Please don't say that. You sound like—" She paused.

"Like all the other suitors?" he smiled.

She sipped her coffee. "It just sounds so trite, mechanical. I expected more from you, Mr. Quist."

"Why?"

"From things I've heard."

"Don't ever expect to get the truth from hearsay," he advised her. "All right, I'll just say I'm very pleased to have a handsome young woman seated across from me. I'll admit, too, that I hoped you'd come to my table eventually. Is that better?"

"It sounds more natural, at least. Mr. Quist, what have you been hearing about me? I know people talk in a town like this, and being a divorcée, it's bound to happen."

Quist shrugged. "Nothing much. I hear you're very popular with a number of men. I find nothing wrong with that. Apparently—"

"Good heavens, Greg Quist, what is a woman to do? I like to get out and get around. If somebody takes me to an entertainment or riding, immediately the gossips' tongues start wagging. Why, when I went to work for Mr. Inwood, a number of people were shocked. It seems they felt that no woman should be doing a job of this sort. I'm proud of my work; I feel I've accomplished something here." She added, "And I'm not ready to again get married. So must I become a recluse?"

"Not at all, Mrs. Monroe. I think you have the correct attitude. Gossip? Just accept it as a compliment. I've never yet known an unattractive woman to arouse gossip."

"That's one of the nicest things anyone ever said to me," she told him. Then she changed the subject abruptly. "I hear you had some trouble this afternoon up in the mountains. You and Scott Fletcher."

"Where'd you hear that?"

"It's all over town. I don't remember who told me. I saw Cody Hayden in the lobby a little while ago. Maybe it was Cody who said something about it. It might be wise, Mr. Quist, to be very careful."

"Why do you say that?"

"If I knew you better, I might tell you. As it is— well, perhaps Sheriff Beadle doesn't welcome another lawman coming here."

"You mean that Beadle arranged for some ambushing?"

"Heavens, no! I wouldn't know a thing about it. But there is bound to be some resentment when a new man comes here. Especially one with your reputation. How do you like Scott Fletcher?"

"He's okay in my book. Why?"

"I'm glad you like him. I've always felt sorry for Scott—his father dying that way and losing his ranch

—and all and going to prison. Somehow I've always felt he had a better deal due him."

"What are you trying to tell me, Mrs. Monroe?"

She didn't answer that, but rose abruptly to her feet. "I've got to rush. There're things to see to in the kitchen. I'll see you again, Mr. Quist."

She was hurriedly leaving the room, even as Quist rose from his chair. He settled back, frowning, "Now what in the devil was she hinting at?" A Mexican girl was extinguishing the lamps at one side of the room. Quist took the hint, tossed some money on the table and made his way out to the hotel gallery.

XIV

He crossed the road and sauntered down to the sheriff's office.

Beadle and Jeff Crawford were engaged in serious conversation when Quist arrived. They broke off at his entrance. Beadle looked up without saying anything. The deputy said, "Evening, Greg. How's it going?"

Quist gave them a small confident smile. "Better than I thought." Though uninvited he pulled a chair toward him and sat down. "It's funny how things work out," he commented carelessly. "I walk around, drop a question here and there. I get answers and put them together. Finally I begin to learn things."

"What do you mean by that, Quist?" Beadle asked nervously. "What kind of things?"

"Oh, various things. Y'know, the more I talk the more Scott Fletcher gets my sympathy."

"In what way?" from Crawford.

"In all ways. I'm beginning to think he was the victim of a crooked deal. Sheriff, I understand you signed as witness to the sale of Beriah Fletcher's Rafter-F to Webb Monroe."

"That's right," Beadle blustered. "What about it?"

"Would you be willing to swear to that?"

"I already swore to it in a court of law."

"That's right, you did. I'd forgotten. Well, there's nothing more to say then—right at present."

Beadle looked nervous. "You mean Scott Fletcher intends to get that case reopened?"

"I didn't say that," Quist offered casually.

Beadle's face grew red. "By God, if he tried to do that, he'd have to offer some fresh evidence."

Quist laughed easily. "We're well aware of that, sheriff."

"You mean you've uncovered some fresh evidence?" Beadle blurted.

"I didn't say that either," Quist laughed. The sheriff looked nonplused. "Oh, by the way," Quist continued, "do you still want that old bow? I had a chance to look it over—"

"We'd be obliged, Greg, if you'd let us have it," Crawford cut in quickly.

"Afraid I can't do it," Quist explained. "Somebody wanted it worse than you did. I had it wrapped in newspapers in my room and somebody stole it—"

"That wasn't—" Beadle started and abruptly checked the words.

"Wasn't what?" Quist asked.

Beadle said lamely, "That bow wasn't necessary any longer. I decided not to investigate that skeleton. Probably just one of those lousy Tonkawas that used to be around here—"

"You're right there, sheriff," Quist nodded pleasantly. "It was Nick, the Tonkawa—you know, the Injun that used to follow Beriah Fletcher around like a dog. Faithful cuss. I guess he knew a lot that went on—"

"About what?" Beadle asked.

Quist's shoulders lifted in a careless shrug. "Why ask me, sheriff? I wasn't here when Beriah Fletcher was murdered."

Beadle's head was dotted with perspiration. "Most folks think that Fletcher was killed by Tonkawas—Nick's pals."

"I've heard of that. Were moccasin tracks or boot tracks found near Fletcher's place up at Tourmaline when the murder was discovered?"

Beadle was silent. "We-ell, I suppose so—never gave it any thought—"

"Yet you went up there and investigated the murder didn't you, sheriff?"

"Certain I did," Beadle snapped testily.

"And yet you didn't see any moccasin tracks. I've been sort of wondering about that. Now I know."

Beadle lost his temper. "God damn it, Quist, what are you getting at?"

"Take it easy, Mort," Crawford said sharply.

"Why I'm not getting at anything in particular," Quist said genially. "Just asking questions and finding out things, like I told you I'd been doing. Cripes! I didn't come in here to make talk. I'm ready to talk to Tilford and Sheldon, though. I suppose they're in cells—"

"You can't talk to them," Beadle snapped, once more on sure ground.

"That's right, Greg," Crawford affirmed. "Doc Nash said they weren't to be bothered until they're a mite better. You can ask Doc if you don't believe us."

"Hey now, why shouldn't I believe you? I can at least swear to warrants, now, anyway."

Beadle shook his head. "We'd have no go before Judge Perkins—he's the J.P. here—in the morning and get the warrant. And I'm not sure he'll hold court tomorrow. I heard he was ailing. No rush about it, is there, Quist?"

Quist rose to his feet. "It's up to you, sheriff. The sooner things are settled the better it might be all around. And in case you can think of anything else related to Beriah Fletcher's murder, just let me know. I'll be more than glad to hear anything you have to say. It might save me digging around some more, and digging is work. Somehow, though, it turns up things. So long, gentlemen—"

"Just a minute, Quist," Crawford protested. Beadle appeared unable to speak; his eyes were wide, his jaw hanging. "There seems to be a double meaning in your words. We'd like some explanation of what you're getting at."

"Oh, yes, that reminds me. Double meaning? All right, I'll speak more plainly, Jeff. Didn't I understand you were a deputy in Puma County before the sheriff appointed you here?"

"That's right."

"Damn funny," Quist scowled.

"What is?"

"I had our office run you down a bit. There's no record in Puma County of a Deputy Jeff Crawford ever having worked there. And our office doesn't make mistakes. Again, good night, gentlemen."

Neither man replied as Quist rose and strolled out of the sheriff's office.

He cut diagonally across Trail Street, musing. Maybe that will give them both something to think about. If I'm not badly mistaken, Beadle knows more about Beriah Fletcher's case than he's told. A little more pressure and he might break, if I can just keep on tossing out a bluff now and then.

Lights and loud voices, the clinking of glasses sounded from the War-Drum Saloon. Quist pushed on through the pair of batwing doors and stepped inside. He paused a moment, looking over the place. Most of Monroe's Diamond-M Connected crew seemed on hand, Vink Fisher among them. Near the center of the bar, Cody Hayden and Webb Monroe stood talking. Hayden seemed slightly unsteady on his feet and his eyes were bloodshot.

". . . and I'm telling you, Webb," he was saying thickly, "that there's got to be a showdown between me and Mort Beadle. He acts like he's a big boss here, or something—"

"Sure, sure, Cody," Monroe said' in soothing tones, "but why bother me with it? I'm not Mort's keeper—" He paused, noting that Quist was standing, listening, just within the entrance.

Quist went to the bar and asked for a cigar when the barkeep arrived to ascertain his wants. He lighted it, placed money on the bar and waited. Within a few minutes, Monroe joined him.

"Better have one of my smokes, Mr. Quist," he offered. "The cigars here aren't of the best."

"Thanks, no, I'll put up with this," Quist said. He sniffed at his cigar. "I just dropped in for a minute. Thought I might find Mead Guthrie here."

"Mead left not ten minutes before you came in. No, I don't know where he was going. He said he hoped to see you around town someplace. Maybe he headed for the hotel. Matter of fact, I wanted to see you on the same matter. You and Scott Fletcher had a little run in with one of my men. I don't quite get what it was all about, and neither does Guthrie. I don't understand what Tilford and Sheldon were doing up in the mountains this afternoon—"

"Have you asked them?"

"I intended to talk to Tilford, but Doc Nash gave orders nobody was to bother either him or Sheldon. I guess that Guthrie was told the same thing when he wanted to see Sheldon. Exactly what happened?"

"The two of 'em tried to ambush Scott Fletcher and me and got the worst of it," Quist said shortly. "They handed out some sort of song-and-dance about mistaking us for two other hombres. Buffalo chips, of course."

"I don't know," Monroe frowned. "It's possible they made a mistake. Maybe you and Fletcher were over hasty."

"You have to be with slugs whining around your ears," Quist snapped. "What would you have done in a like situation?"

Monroe didn't reply to that. He said, "Mort Beadle says you want a warrant and arrest for those two men. I'm telling you now, Quist, that I'll offer bail the instant they're arrested."

"That I'd expect," Quist said quietly. "A man has to protect his own interests."

"Exactly what do you mean by that?" Monroe flared.

"Why, not a thing, Monroe." Quist laughed softly. "Naturally you'd want Tilford back working for you as soon as possible. Isn't that taking care of your interests?"

"Oh—oh, I see." Monroe appeared somewhat confused. "Fact is, you and I seem to be working at cross-purposes. You've shot one of my men, and yesterday you made a fool out of another."

"I didn't make a fool out of Vink Fisher if that's what you mean. He always was a fool—and something worse. I'm surprised that an honest cowman would hire Fisher."

"Could be you're right," Monroe conceded. "But I needed a hand and when he showed up I hired him. He's a good worker."

"That I doubt, if you're referring to punching cows, Quist said flatly. He turned and called down the bar, "Fisher, come here a minute."

Fisher stepped back from his group then paused. "You want me, Webb?"

"Quist does," Monroe said shortly.

Reluctantly, Fisher approached. One of Monroe's men called after him, "You're safe, Vink. He hasn't a bottle of beer." The remark brought forth considerable laughter.

"What do you want, Quist?" Fisher said in ugly tones.

"Mr. Monroe tells me you're a good worker, Fisher. What's your job?"

Fisher looked to Monroe for a cue, but Monroe didn't say anything. "Oh,—uh—I work—I dig irrigation ditches and rope cows and string fences and—well, I just sort of—"

"Yeah, you just 'sort of'," Quist sneered. He seized Fisher's right hand and before the man could jerk away, ran fingers over the palm. "No, no calluses. So that makes you a liar too, Fisher."

"What in hell you think you're doing, Quist?" Fisher protested. He looked to Monroe for help.

Monroe snapped, "Take it easy, Quist. I won't have my men pushed around in such fashion."

"Call your choice then, Monroe. Exactly what fashion do you prefer? Because they're sure as hell going to be pushed around, if they don't watch their step. And you too, Monroe."

"What in hell you getting at, Quist?"

"I'm trying to find out whether it was you or Fisher hired two pot-shooters to try and rub us out this afternoon."

"Oh, now look here, Quist," Monroe started, "you can't imagine I had anything to do—"

"You can count me out on that score, Quist," Fisher snarled. "All right, I've got a score to settle with you, but, mister, I do my own settling. You'll see!"

Quist laughed suddenly. "By God, I think you're just fool enough to try it, too, Fisher."

Fisher swung angrily away and rejoined his pals. Monroe looked rather pale. "Quist, you're acting like you want trouble."

"Isn't that the quickest way to bring things to a head?"

"But, why? I don't want any fuss with you. All I ask is to be friends. You come raging into town. You've got Mort Beadle all stirred up. You throw accusations around—I swear to you I know nothing about that attempted ambush today. Why should I want you killed? Or Fletcher?"

"I've not said yet that you did, Monroe."

"You as much as said so."

Quist laughed. "I was just fishing for information. Maybe I got more than you thought."

He nodded shortly to Monroe and strolled out of the War-Drum leaving a puzzled-looking Monroe staring after him.

"And now," Quist muttered as he reached the street, "maybe I've given Monroe something to bother him."

He was just passing the closed Rosebud Opera House when Jeff Crawford hailed him from across the street. Quist waited while the deputy closed the intervening yards between them. He said without preliminary, "You sure got me in a hell of a jam, Greg, but maybe I had it coming."

"Maybe you did," Quist said gravely.

"Mort's been giving me merry hell. So by tomorrow maybe I won't be wearing this deputy badge. To tell the truth, when I came here, I was broke. I needed the job bad. Mort didn't question it when I lied and told him I'd held a job as deputy in Puma County. All's I hoped was to get a few bucks to carry me along until he checked on my story, but he never did get around to checking and I stayed on the job. I've done my best here and nobody's had any kick—least of all, Mort. But he can't get over being deceived."

"In a way, you can't blame him, Jeff," Quist pointed out in kindly tones. Crawford agreed with that. "Anyway, Jeff, you've got it off your chest now, and you have nothing more to be afraid of, whether he fires you or not."

"Sure, you're right, Greg. I just made one damn fool move, and maybe now I'll have to pay for it."

"Want I should go over and put in a good word for you?"

"Would you?"—eagerly. Then, "No, better wait until Mort cools down. He'll be more ready to listen to reason tomorrow."

"Probably you're right. Well, I'll see you tomorrow, then."

They said good night and Quist proceeded on his way. He had progressed a half-block when he turned in time to see Crawford enter the War-Drum Saloon. "Looks like the deputy is in need of a drink right now," Quist chuckled.

He crossed the street and from the vantage of a recessed doorway of a darkened store stood watching for a few minutes. He was about to give up and return to the hotel when he spied Jeff Crawford and Webb Monroe leave the saloon. The two stood talking at the War-Drum tierail for several minutes, the light from the saloon window throwing their forms into bold relief. Once Quist saw Monroe pounding one fist angrily into the other. Crawford seemed to be putting up some sort of protest and they argued for several minutes. Eventually, they appeared to quiet down, turned and re-entered the saloon together.

"Now, I wonder what that was all about?" Quist scowled. He stood, considering the business a minute, then emerged from his hiding place and returned to the hotel. Fifteen minutes later he was asleep in his bed.

XV

"Sheriff Beadle committed suicide sometime during the night."

"Hell's-bells on a tomcat! You're sure?"

"Oh, it's certain all right. Several men have told me—"

Quist didn't wait to hear more, but hurried from the hotel and strode swiftly in the direction of the sheriff's office. A crowd had collected about the entrance. Quist pushed through and entered the open doorway to find Jeff Crawford and Doctor Nash inside. On the floor, to one side of the closed door leading to the cell block at the rear, lay the still figure of Sheriff Beadle, the glazed eyes but partly closed. The sheriff was clothed only in his long underwear, the middle of which was stained darkly. A short distance from the body, the sheriff's gun lay on the floor.

Crawford looked pale. "Isn't this a hell of a thing, Greg? I'm plain buffaloed. Maybe you can advise me."

"I don't know as any advice I can give would help Mort."

"I—uh— mean I just never had any experience with anything like this before—"

"When did it happen?" Quist asked.

"We're not certain. Doc Nash figures it must have been about three this morning. One of the prisoners in the cells says he thought he heard a shot last night, but he was half-asleep and has no idea what time it was. He didn't give it any thought. Nor, I suppose, did anybody else who might have heard it. Every so often some cowpunch leaving town with a skinful lets loose a shot or so to wake up the town—"

Doctor Nash cut in, "Well, there's nothing else I can do, Jeff. As town coroner I think we'd better hold the inquest as soon as possible. Say this afternoon about three. You can doubtless round up a coroner's jury for me by that time, can't you? And try to dig up any witnesses that might have seen Mort last, if possible."

"I just can't believe that Mort's gone." Crawford appeared stunned. "Oh, sure, Doc. I'll try to have things ready for you. This sort of hits me where it hurts." He brushed at his eyes with the back of his hand. "What about the body?"

"I'll send somebody down to the undertaker's. More'n likely Flannery has already heard about it and will be here shortly, but I'll see to it. Then I'm going to grab a nap."

"Right, thanks, Doc." The doctor nodded to Quist and took his departure, carrying his black bag.

Crawford turned helplessly to Quist. "God, I don't know where to start."

"You're certain it was suicide?"

Crawford looked startled. "Why, what else could it be? I don't see how it could be anything else. Mort didn't have any enemies. Not enemies that would kill him, leastwise. I don't think so, anyway."

"When did you last talk to him?"

"Last night. After I left you, I needed a drink. I dropped into the War-Drum. Webb Monroe was there. I told him about my trouble with Mort and asked him to put in a good word for me. He and I came out to the hitchrack and talked it over. There was too much noise in the barroom. Monroe sort of bawled me out for lying about having a job in Puma, but he said he'd talk to Mort this morning." He broke off as some of the crowd was edging up on the porch and swung the door to. Then he returned to the center of the room, saying,

"I had another drink with Webb, then came back here. Mort had cooled down some, but he wasn't in any friendly mood. I said I guessed I'd go to my rooming house and turn in if he didn't need me. He told me to suit myself, so I headed for bed. Lord, I hate to think that we parted on an unfriendly basis."

"Well, it's something that can't be helped. No use you brooding about it, Jeff."

"I reckon not, but it's going to be hard to forget. Anyway, I figured to get here about seven this morning and talk things out with Mort. The door was closed when I got here. Locked from inside. I figured Mort was still asleep on his cot. I looked through the window and saw him sprawled on the floor. Never figured him as being dead. He wasn't old enough for a stroke or anything of the kind. Thought he was probably sick. So then I started to force the door—"

"Don't you have a key?"

Crawford shook his head. "There's never been but the one key since I've been deputy. Half the time Mort didn't bother to lock the door when he turned in. But this time it was locked tight, on the inside. I still didn't suspect anything like this. Many's the time I've come early and walked in and Mort was just waking—"

"So you had to force the lock."

"Yes, and what a job that was. That's a tough old door and lock. I'd thrown my shoulder against it once, but it wouldn't give. About that time Rick Kincaid—he runs the post office down to the stage station—came along and asked what I was doing. I told him and he gave me a hand. Together we managed to break in, with the door jamb being ripped loose before we made it. Mort was already dead, though, the gun still gripped in his hand. I started out for the doctor, though I knew it wasn't much use. Lucky Doc Nash was just passing by when I stepped out, returning from an early morning call. He examined the body and told Rick and me what we already knew—that Mort was done for. Why do you suppose he did it, Greg?"

Quist frowned. "Lord knows, but I've a hunch that the sheriff had too much on his mind. I figured him at the breaking point, Jeff, and he had to tell what he knew or—do what he did."

"T'hell you say! But what could be wrong?"

"Maybe he had a bad conscience."

"I don't know why he should have," the deputy said dubiously. "He's been mixed in no trouble—that is, since I've been here. 'Course at one time he expected to marry Mrs. Monroe, but Cody Hayden stepped in. I remember they had words, and Mort knocked him down—but that wouldn't lead to this."

"He didn't leave a note or anything?"

"I looked around after Doc Nash took over, but I couldn't find anything of the sort. It's sure got me guessing. Look here, Greg, I've got to get out and persuade some men to act on the coroner's jury. Would you mind staying around here for a spell?"

"Sure, go ahead, Jeff. Don't hurry. There's enough fellows peering in at the windows now. Maybe you'll not have to go far."

"Fat chance. They'll all alibi that they have their regular jobs to go to. I'll see you later." Crawford opened the door and pulled it closed. It sagged a little and wouldn't remain tightly shut. Quist heard the deputy talking to the men outside and they started to disperse.

Quist gazed down at the still form of the sheriff. "So maybe you couldn't take it any more, eh, sheriff?" he muttered. He stooped by the body, closely looking it over, talking half-aloud to himself. "I wish I could have been here before the doctor took over. He must have taken the gun from the hand and straightened out the body while making his examination."

Quist reached across and picked up the six-shooter. The cylinder contained two exploded shells and four loaded cartridges, Quist found upon examination. One of the exploded shells had rested beneath the firing pin; the other was a trifle corroded and had probably been in the gun a long time. "Likely," Quist speculated, "Beadle carried his hammer on an empty shell like most cow-country folks." He replaced the cylinder in the position he had found it and put the gun back on the floor.

"I don't know," he grunted, "what to think. Jeff said Beadle was still gripping the gun when they found the body. A shot plumb center like this is mighty painful and a man doesn't die instantly. I sort of wonder—if he did it himself—if Beadle would have been interested in hanging on to his gun at that moment. I'd be more inclined to think he'd drop the gun and grab his belly with both hands. But I can't be sure."

He drew back the unbuttoned upper half of the underwear and studied the wound, then recovered it with the muttered remark that "a forty-five can sure play hell. If it was a forty-five. That hole was right large caliber anyway."

He glanced toward the window. Men still stood talking on the sidewalk, but no one was looking inside at the moment. Quist edged the corpse on its side and scanned the back of the body from bare toes to head. The hair was long at the back. Quist ran his fingers lightly through it, then paused abruptly. One finger had encountered something slightly rough and swollen. Quist spread the hairs and stooped closer, seeing now a tiny cut in the scalp and a bit of dried blood. The small wound had bled scarcely at all and appeared more like a scratch.

"*Hmmm,* I thought so," Quist muttered. "I never figured Beadle had enough courage to kill himself.

He was the type that would have squealed first. It looks like this might have been done to keep his mouth shut. Someone came in here during the night and knocked him on the head, then shot Beadle with the sheriff's own gun. That blow on the head wasn't too heavy. Probably it just landed hard enough to stun Beadle momentarily. Could be a gunbarrel was used. And Doc Nash, tired like he was from his night call, never noticed this mark beneath the hair. I'm not surprised."

Gently, Quist allowed the corpse to roll back to its former position, and got to his feet. "Some one came in here,"—speaking half-aloud, a deep frown on his face—"and killed Beadle. It's murder, not suicide. Wait a sec, Quist. Jeff said that door was locked on the inside. The key was still in the lock when they broke in. Even if the murderer had a second key, he wouldn't have been able to lock the door when he left—not and leave a key on the inside of the lock. Damn! This is going to require some figuring."

He frowned around the room, noticing the cot with its rumpled blankets, and the sheriff's boots on the floor. His gaze strayed to a hook in the wall where hung the sheriff's cartridge belt and empty holster. Quist crossed to the sheriff's desk and examined the lamp. The oil in its base was nearly gone. "So he must have sat late talking to somebody, somebody who was persuading him not to do any squealing. The persuasion didn't work so the killer returned later and really shut Beadle's mouth—wait a minute, Quist. You're jumping to conclusions. Maybe there's an unlocked back door."

Scowling, he went to the door of the cell block, unlocked it and passed on through between the rows of cells, four on each side. He went to the end and found himself against a blank wall. There was no rear door to the building. Therefore, the murderer had had to enter and leave by the front door. But how in the devil had he been able to do that, lock the door, and still leave the key in the lock, *on the inside?* It wasn't a snap lock; the latch had to be manually operated.

Quist turned and headed back toward the office. A couple of prisoners in cells stared at him, without speaking. On the other side, two cells farther on, Tilford and Sheldon were stretched lazily on cots. Tilford was sleeping, but Sheldon raised his head. "Quist, I heard Beadle bumped himself off last night. What about—?"

"That's what I heard too," Quist replied without stopping.

He passed through into the office, relocked the cell. block door and went to the front door, which stood closed as far as it would go. Part of the doorjamb sagged to one side where it had been wrenched loose; broken and bent screws dangled loosely from its catch plate. He turned his attention to the lock, from the keyhole of which the key still protruded in the locked position, its latch extended beyond the doorplate. He opened the door, glanced at the outside keyhole, but that offered no ready solution. Closing the door again, he withdrew the key and studied it. It was close to four inches long and showed the usage of years, its metal surface covered with a thin rust over the part that rested within the lock.

One point stood out: the lock had apparently been recently oiled, a bit of the oil on the key coming off on Quist's fingers. "Anyway," Quist mused, "somebody wanted to make sure this key turned easily in its lock—"

He paused suddenly, noticing something else that had hitherto escaped his attention; the end of the keypin, just beyond the bit, had a number of tiny scratches where the brighter metal shone through the slightly rusted, oily surface. Quist whistled softly. Things were coming clearer now. He started to replace the key, then, instead, slipped it into one pocket.

"So that's how it was done," he told himself. "The killer struck Beadle on the head first, so he couldn't put up a fight. Then he got the sheriff's gun and shot him. Next he placed the gun in the man's hand. That done, he left, closed the door and through the outside keyhole turned the key until it was locked. Now all I've got to do is find out how he reached the key from *the outside keyhole*. And that's going to take some more thinking."

He was seated on a chair, mind deep in thought, when Jeff Crawford returned, a number of men trailing him. Jeff closed the door in their faces and dropped wearily into another chair. "Whew! That's done. Damn! The questions I've had to answer."

"What sort of questions?"

The deputy shrugged. "You know, just idle questions about Mort. He's going to be missed. Most folks liked him a heap—"

"What folks didn't? Can you name any?"

"Oh, I don't know,"—frowning—"Cody Hayden for one, Mead Guthrie. I think Merle Inwood was jealous of him too. Webb Monroe was sort of riled at Mort because Mort put Tilford in a cell, but what else could Mort do? Anyway, a cell's the best place for him, so long as he has to have Doc Nash's attention. There's no place in town takes care of wounded men." He cast a sidelong glance at the still form on the floor. "The undertaker's promised to come right along, but he's taking a hell of a time to get here."

"Get your coroner's jury picked out?"

Jeff nodded. "I picked from men who were here shortly after I broke in the door, men who had had a chance to see the body and how it laid, with the gun in hand and everything. So that should help matters and speed up the inquest. I don't figure it will take long. Will you attend?"

"Any particular reason why I should?" Quist asked.

"Not unless you can give evidence of some sort."

"I can't think of a thing I'd want to say now. Did you find anybody who might have been the last one to talk with the sheriff?"

"Nary a man. Anyway, no one would want to admit he'd talked to Mort, a short time before Mort blew himself wide open. And I was in my bed."

A noise was heard at the door, and a man peered within. "Stay out, whoever you are," Crawford snapped. The face disappeared. "Never seen so many people with a morbid curiosity," Crawford crabbed. "If Flannery wasn't coming after the body, I'd lock that door and—" He broke off, gazing in the direction of the door.

"What's up?" Quist asked, his face blank.

"The key's gone from the lock."

"Key? Oh, the doorkey. Likely you knocked it out when you busted in the door."

"I could have sworn it stayed in the lock." Looking somewhat perturbed, Crawford got down on hands and knees and began to search about the floor, muttering to himself. A wagon drew up before the tierail outside, and Quist said he guessed it was the undertaker arriving at last. Crawford rose to his feet. "Yeah, that's Flannery. Wonder where that key got to? Oh, well, I guess it doesn't matter. Doc Nash saw it in the lock when he first arrived."

"Maybe some hombre grabbed it out of the keyhole," Quist suggested.

"Why should he?" Crawford asked.

Quist shrugged. "Souvenir, perhaps; you know, one of those morbid fellers you mentioned."

Crawford's face clouded, "It would be just like one of those bastards to do just that—" He paused as the door was pushed open and the undertaker followed by an assistant entered, bearing a stretcher. Quist started to work his way past, headed for the door.

"I'll see you later, Jeff," he said in farewell. The deputy, busied with the undertaker, gave him only a brief nod.

"My next move," he decided, "is to wash a bit of town dust from my throat." He turned in at the hotel and mounting the steps crossed the gallery to the hotel bar entrance. Small knots of men stood here and there along the bar, speaking interestedly of the sheriff.

Quist headed for the far end where there was relative seclusion. Keg Hooper came down the bar a minute later with a bottle of beer.

"Some shock, eh, Mr. Quist?" he commented.

"Sudden, all right," Quist agreed.

"What do you suppose made Mort do it?" Hooper asked.

"Find the last man to see him alive and he might have a story to tell."

"Who would that be?"

"That's what Jeff Crawford is trying to find out now."

Hooper went away to attend a customer's needs, then returned. He said low voiced, "Last night after I closed up, I took a walk to get some fresh air. As I passed the sheriff's office I saw Webb Monroe inside. I walked on out Trail to the end of the street. When I came back, Webb was gone, but Mead Guthrie was talking to the sheriff. They looked to be arguing about something. Didn't think anything about it, of course."

"What time was that?"

"Around one-thirty this morning."

"See anybody else?"

"Trail was pretty well deserted. I do remember seeing Cody Hayden come out of the War-Drum. Cody was carrying a load and had a hard time getting into his saddle, but he made it. Last I saw him, he was heading out east on Trail. Say, do you suppose I ought to tell Crawford about seeing Monroe and Guthrie with the sheriff?"

Quist looked at the bartender, then shrugged. "Suit yourself."

Keg Hooper returned the look. "All right, I'll just forget it for the time being."

Quist finished his beer, strolled out of the barroom and crossed to the Flying Hooves Livery where he had the buckskin saddled. Once mounted, he headed out of town and took the trail that ran to the Bench-G Ranch. *I figure it's about time I had some straight talk with Mead Guthrie,* Quist told himself.

XVI

Mead Guthrie was seated on the gallery nursing a smelly brier pipe when Quist rode up, the man's feet propped on a second chair. He glowered at Quist, nodded shortly and said "Howdy."

Quist sat his saddle, looking down on the big man. He said quietly, "Do I get an invitation to 'light?"

"Suit yourself," Guthrie said ungraciously. He poked one finger into the bowl of his brier. "Any particular reason for you coming here?"

Quist got down from his horse and dropped the reins on the ground. He stepped up on the porch, seized a vacant chair nearby and dropped onto it. "Webb Monroe said last night you wanted to see me. I figured you and I might have one or two things to talk over—"

"You're damn right I want to see you," Guthrie exploded, as though he'd held in long enough. "Ain't no man going to war on one of my hands and not have to answer to me. Scott Fletcher is going to have to answer for shooting that arrow into Sheldon—"

Quist cut in sharply, "You'd best cool down and listen to some reasoning before you get an attack of apoplexy, Guthrie. Stall if you like, but you'd better face a few facts—"

"Don't bother trying to lie to me, Quist. I'll—"

"Look here, Guthrie, if you were riding along, minding your own business, and somebody fired on you, what would you do?"

"By Gawd, I'd blast the dirty son—"

"That's what Scott and I did."

"It's my notion that you and Fletcher jumped 'em."

"Why should we?"

"Fletcher's always been a troublemaker—"

"I don't agree with that, but maybe he's had reason. Suppose somebody cheated you out of your ranch—"

"Now, look here, Quist, that was all fair and aboveboard—"

"Buffalo chips!" Quist spat contemptuously.

"What do you mean by that?" Guthrie said quickly.

"We'll get to that presently. I've told you how I feel

153

about Sheldon and Tilford. If you try to protect them you'll get your ass in a sling—"

"By Gawd, you're as overbearing as Mort Beadle. Wouldn't even let me talk to my own hand, last evening. Doctor's orders, he says. Yaah! One of these days Beadle and I are due for a showdown—"

"No you're not."

"What do you mean by that?"

"Nobody's been here with any news then?"

"What sort of news? What you hitting at, Quist?"

"Mort Beadle's dead."

Guthrie's jaw dropped. He stared uncomprehendingly at Quist. Then slowly, "Who killed him?"

"What gives you the idea somebody did?"

"Well—er—he had enemies—"

"Who?"

"Well, I wouldn't want to name ary man in particular. He and Webb Monroe had had run ins 'bout one thing and another. Cody Hayden. He knocked Cody down once. I don't know . . ."

"I've heard it said you and the sheriff had your unfriendly moments. Some jealousy over a lady, wasn't it?"

Guthrie's face turned purple. "Now, you look here, Quist—" He stopped suddenly, then, "All right, maybe I did have a couple of fool ideas, one time, but I was never real serious."

"Forget it," Quist said in bored accents. "I didn't see you around town last night."

"I was there. I sort of drifted around to different

saloons, talked to fellers about one thing or another."

"What time did you get home?"

Guthrie scowled and started to refill his pipe. He tamped down the tobacco and lighted it. Then, "I don't figure it was much after ten. Why?"

"You were seen talking to the sheriff about two this morning."

"That's a lie!"

"I don't think so, Guthrie."

"All right, maybe it was later than I thought when I got home. Sure, I talked to the sheriff. When he won't allow me to talk to one of my own hands—doctor's orders, or no doctor's orders—it makes me plumb riled. Sa-a-ay"—a sudden thought striking him—"you ain't thinking I had anything to do with Mort's death?"

"Don't get your rear end in a fret. I didn't even hint at anything of the sort. Fact is, they're calling it suicide—"

"Suicide!" There was a note of relief in Guthrie's voice. "All right. Tell it."

"There's not much to tell—yet. Jeff Crawford arrived at the office this morning and found Beadle dead, with his own gun clenched in his fist. The door had been locked on the inside."

"I'll be damned! I reckon I'd best saddle up and ride on in. I won't say as how Mort and I always saw eye to eye—but now he's dead, I don't hold grudges. When's the funeral?"

"I don't know. There's an inquest at three today."

Guthrie consulted his watch. "I could make it. if I hurried."

"Maybe that's an idea. They're looking for someone who might have talked to him last."

"Guess I wouldn't have time after all. I'll swear I don't understand what come over Mort. He was acting worried when I saw him, and then he got mad when he and I took to arguing. I finally left—but, say, that's too damn bad. In some ways I liked Mort right well. I'll go to his funeral—"

There was a step at the open door leading to the gallery, and Sheila Guthrie stepped out, carrying a tray with sandwiches. The girl wore a white shirtwaist and dark skirt. Her auburn hair was done high on her head. "I heard you out here, Mr. Quist. It was time for Dad to have a bite so I figured you'd be hungry too."

Quist was already on his feet, hat in hand. Guthrie looked suspiciously at the girl. "When did you meet Quist?" he demanded.

"A couple of days back, up at Scott Fletcher's place—"

"Damn it, girl! You been up there again?" His face grew red.

"I told you I wasn't going to be bossed around any longer," Sheila said defiantly.

"By Gawd, girl, I'll—" Guthrie stopped, holding himself in check. "No need to do our washing in public," he growled. "Sheila, you and me will talk this over later."

"It's settled as far as I'm concerned," the girl said

shortly, then, "here, take this tray before I drop it. Greg, I'll take your horse down to the corral and have one of the boys water it."

"I'll be obliged," Quist said.

The girl gathered the reins and led the horse around the corner of the house. Guthrie gazed resentfully after her until she'd disappeared. "What can you do with a woman like that?" he growled.

"What can you do with women?" Quist laughed.

"You had trouble with 'em too?"

"Who hasn't?"

There was little talk while they ate the sandwiches. There was a bottle of beer for Quist and whisky and water for Guthrie. Finished, Quist rolled a cigarette. Guthrie jammed fresh tobacco in his pipe. "Should've told Sheila about Mort Beadle," he grunted. "She'd be mighty surprised." *Puff, puff.* "Don't like her running off to see Scott Fletcher. I already forbid her."

"What you got against Fletcher?"

"Didn't he try to kill me once? Wasn't his father a crook?"

"No. On both counts."

"What do you mean by that?"

"As I understand it, you must have been expecting trouble with Scott that day. You had a bodyguard of two men and they tried to take care of him—"

"Gawd dammit!" Guthrie roared. "I didn't have no such thing. Those two were just a couple of cow-punchers I'd hired that day. When they saw Fletcher start to gun me, they tried to stop him, as any hand would do for an employer. Maybe they were a mite hasty, but if you knew Fletcher and his father—"

"How'd you happen to find those two cowhands on that particular day, Guthrie?"

"Webb Monroe recommended 'em to me. They were just a couple of footloose cowhands looking for a job."

"Where'd you get Bert Sheldon?"

"Sheldon? Why, uh, he used to work for Monroe. Monroe had to lay him off and he said he was a good man and I hired him. Worked all right too."

"How many other hands have you hired on Monroe's recommendation?"

"Hell, I don't know. I have a hard time keeping men—"

"Maybe they don't like to be yelled at. So from time to time when a man quits, Monroe always seems to be laying one off. Is that the case?"

Guthrie frowned. "We-ell, it might look that way, but I reckon it's just coincidence."

"I'm not so sure. I've a hunch that Monroe has infiltrated your crew for a long time. Ever lose any cows?"

"Show me a stock raiser who hasn't. But not like I was losing when Beriah Fletcher was running the Rafter-F. What are you driving at Quist?"

"I think you've been played for a sucker, Guthrie."

Guthrie thundered, "I demand your reason for that statement!"

"You'll get it," Quist said quietly. "Let's think things over according to information I've picked up. Webb

Monroe came to this country with practically nothing. Next thing, he had a going outfit. Where'd he get his cows? Not only that, his herds fluctuate in size. You said yourself he's always laying off hands—and then turning them over to you—"

"This is hard to believe," Guthrie scowled. "I—"

"Don't believe then, if you want to be bullheaded. Monroe feared suspicion might fall on him, so he rigged the game by branding some of your calves with Fletcher's Rafter-F brand. And like a fool you fell for the trap and yanked your gun on Beriah Fletcher. So there, Monroe made bad feeling between the two of you. Could he have promoted a real range war, neither of you would have had any' cows left by the time it was settled. But Fletcher was too level-headed to be pulled into trouble of that sort."

"You claimin' I wronged Beriah Fletcher?" Guthrie bristled.

"I sure as hell am! Particularly when you found you couldn't buy Fletcher out, so you gave Monroe twenty thousand and hired him to get the ranch so he could turn it over to you—"

"How the hell did you learn that? If Monroe told you—"

"Thanks," Quist smiled. "I was just making a good guess, but now I know it happened that way. The ranch was later transferred to you, wasn't it?"

"Sure," Guthrie snapped. "It wasn't illegal for me to buy the Rafter-F through Monroe."

"I didn't say it was illegal. Just stupid. So when

things were settled and the court had awarded Monroe ownership of the ranch, you bought it from him—at a profit, I suppose, over the fifty thousand he claimed he paid Beriah Fletcher."

"Five thousand profit and I'd already given Monroe five hundred to handle the deal." Guthrie had sobered considerably.

"Didn't it ever occur to you to question where Monroe got the thirty thousand to make up the fifty thousand he claimed to have paid Beriah Fletcher? Everyone knew he was broke most of the time."

Guthrie nodded slightly. "It did seem a mite odd, but it wasn't none of my business where he got his money. All I wanted was the ranch. The deal must have been on the square. Hell, Monroe had the paper signed by Fletcher and witnessed by Mort Beadle, showing he had paid fifty thousand to Fletcher, as the price of the Rafter-F. Why, Mort Beadle swore to it in court too. Told how he had watched Beriah Fletcher count out the fifty thousand before signing. And the court awarded the ranch to Monroe and then he sold it to me."

"That's just a lot of cactus juice," Quist snapped. "What happened to the fifty thousand?"

"I don't know. Beriah's foremen and a couple of his men told in court how they'd seen Beriah and his Injun, Nick, ride off to Tourmaline that day, right after Monroe and Beadle left. As I heard it, Nick and some of his Injun pals raided the place in Tourmaline and killed Fletcher and took the money. Why, there was even an arrow stuck in Fletcher's back. It was fresh painted red. It must have been them redskins."

"God! How gullible can people be?" Quist said savagely. "You're all so greedy to get your own chunk of the boodle that you never pay any attention to what's happening to your neighbor, and a smart crook can make damn fools of you. I'll tell you why the fifty thousand was never found. Webb Monroe never paid Fletcher fifty thousand."

"But—but," Guthrie said dubiously, "Monroe had the bill-of-sale, signed with Fletcher's signature. Witnessed by Mort Beadle."

"It was a forgery."

"The writing was compared to Fletcher's writing on checks. It was the same. The judge saw to that."

"Look, I don't doubt that twenty thousand passed between Monroe and Fletcher. Monroe had the twenty thousand from you. And that twenty thousand hasn't shown up.

"But, you say that paper Monroe had was a forgery. It would take a good hand to forge a signature."

"Let me tell you a story, Guthrie. A short time before Monroe made the deal for the ranch, he came to Fletcher and on the strength of wanting to improve his breed, bought a bull from Beriah Fletcher. He wanted more than one, but Fletcher wouldn't let him have 'em when Monroe said he was too broke to buy more. So Fletcher took his money for one bull and gave him a signed bill-of-sale for the animal. So now, Monroe had Beriah Fletcher's signature, which he could rub on the back with lead pencil, then turn it over and trace Fletcher's signature on a blank sheet of paper. That done he could go over the tracing with ink and then fill in, above, the bill-of-sale for the Rafter-F. Except for the signature the whole paper was written by Monroe, wasn't it?"

Guthrie nodded slowly, eyes worried. "I never heard that about the bull," he said dumbly.

"Naturally," Quist snapped, "because you've heard nothing but a lot of other bull since." He paused. "But Monroe wasn't satisfied with that sort of deal. He had to kill Fletcher to put it across, and he wanted that twenty thousand besides. So Monroe and some others raided the place in Tourmaline and murdered Fletcher and stole the money—though about that last I'm not sure. The stunt with the red arrow was to make folks think Indians were responsible."

"Good Gawd!" Guthrie exploded. "You're making out that Mort Beadle was a crook."

"That's what I'm saying," Quist stated. "A weak link in a crooked chain—so weak he was on the point of doing some squealing when I threw a scare into him with a mite of bluffing."

"So that's why he killed himself." Guthrie's eyes were wide.

"That's why he was murdered," Quist said flatly. "His mouth had to be shut."

"Murdered? Who done it?"

Quist smiled coldly. "I'm naming no names yet, but what were you and Beadle quarreling about last night?"

Guthrie's jaw dropped. "I already told you that, Quist. Gawd dammit! I ain't a killer. Why should I want to kill Mort?"

"To shut his mouth?"

"But why would I want to shut his mouth?"

"Look, Guthrie, if Beadle had told what he knows, the case would have to be reopened in court. How much then do you think your title to the Bench-G would be worth, when it was learned you got the Rafter-F through fraud?"

Guthrie just stared for a few minutes as comprehension slowly came to him. He tried to speak, but choked up. Finally he said hoarsely, "Are you accusing me of killing Mort Beadle?"

"I didn't say that—but you'd have a motive."

"Yes—yes I guess that's so." He swallowed hard. "Look here, Quist, I'm no killer." Quist didn't reply. Guthrie said, "H-h-have you got proof for all you told me?"

"I haven't sewed up all the loose ends yet, Guthrie," Quist evaded. "I told you things as I see them."

"By Gawd, I'm going to find Webb Monroe and question him some. Get to the bottom of this."

"I can't stop you from talking to Monroe, but I doubt you'll get much satisfaction. If you take my advice you'll keep your own mouth shut, until I've brought things to a head. Talk too soon and you may blow things open before I'm ready. And, Guthrie, I don't think you murdered Mort Beadle, if that's any satisfaction."

"Thank Gawd for that, Quist. Maybe I've misjudged you some, but I'll do as you say, keep my mouth shut for the time being."

They talked a few minutes more, then Guthrie accompanied Quist to the corral to get the buckskin. The big man had a stunned expression on his face. Sheila called good-bye as Quist rode past the gallery.

XVII

Quist arrived back in Horcado City around four o'clock, stabled the buckskin and headed for the hotel barroom. The place was crowded with men, all talking of the inquest which had been concluded only some twenty minutes previously. Quist got the verdict through Keg Hooper, while he was sipping a bottle of beer. "Yeah," Keg said, "verdict was suicide. What else could it be, with Mort locked inside his own office? But no one has the least idea why he did it. Reckon he wanted to make a certain job of it, as he'd taken time to slit the end of the slug before shooting himself."

"Where'd you hear that?" Quist asked.

"Doc Nash gave it in his own testimony. He'd performed an autopsy a couple of hours before the inquest was held and probed out the bullet. Doc said it had been slit, split when it hit and really tore a hole in Mort. What do you think of that?"

"I'd say Mort didn't live long after the slug hit. Say, Keg are any of Beriah Fletcher's old hands still on the Bench-G?"

Hooper shook his head. "They all quit after giving testimony in court. None of 'em wanted to work for Guthrie. Don't know where any of them are now. They all drifted out of the country. Why?"

"I was just wondering if the foreman or anybody else happened to be present when Monroe made his deal with Fletcher for the ranch."

"Not according to the testimony I heard. There was just Beriah, Monroe and Mort Beadle there in the house. The crew had no idea what was taking place. They testified that Beriah had taken off for his Tourmaline house, right after they'd seen Monroe and Mort leave, and that Nick, the Tonkawa, was with Beriah."

A short time later, Quist left the barroom. The sun was just dipping behind the Horcados now, throwing long shadows along Trail Street. People were hurrying to their homes, after closing stores. Several wagons and cowponies headed east, west and north out of town. The air was beginning to take on a certain coolness after the heat of the day.

Quist strolled east on Trail Street until he'd reached the sheriff's office. Jeff Crawford was stooped low in the doorway, working at the broken jamb. He straightened up, when Quist spoke to him, and Quist saw he wore on his shirt the sheriff's badge of office. Quist said, "Looks like you've been promoted."

Crawford grinned, coloring slightly. "Yes. The mayor called a quick meeting of the town council and they appointed me sheriff pro tem. I'll like's not finish out Mort's term, and then have to decide if I want to run for office again. You weren't at the inquest this afternoon."

"I don't like inquests, seen too many of 'em. And I had nothing to offer at the time. Heard a verdict of suicide was rendered."

"Couldn't expect anything else. They plan to bury Mort tomorrow. I only hope I can fill his shoes— 'course nobody could really do that, not in my estimation."

Quist left the sidewalk and stepped up on the porch. "What in the devil you working at?"

"Trying to repair this door I busted in this morning. The blasted catchplate is loose, and I've got three of the screws out, but one is broken off short. I've been trying to dig it out of the wood with a knife, but it's plumb rusted in. With the head gone, it's hard to get a grip on."

"Hell, what you need is pliers—and more light."

"Pliers I've got but they're almost too big to grip the edge of the screw. But you're right about the light." He stopped long enough to light the oil lamp."

"Let me hold it for you while you work," Quist offered, then grinned as he saw the pliers Crawford had produced.

"Cripes, you could jerk railroad spikes with those things."

"Ain't it right! Mort got 'em one time to yank a nail out of his horse's shoe, when it went lame. They been kicking around here ever since."

While Quist held the light for Crawford's better visibility, the deputy toiled at the jamb. Finally he removed the plate, which left only a small length of broken screw extending from the wood. As Quist had said the big pliers were almost too large to grip the metal, but by employing one corner of the jaws, Crawford managed it and started to twist the broken bit of threading from its bed. The job was finally done.

"Hmmm," Quist said suddenly.

Crawford looked at him. "What's up?"

"Just had an idea, you could have hired a carpenter to do this job and had it finished by this time."

Crawford shook his head. "If I can get this fixed myself, I'll save the taxpayers that expense. I want to show folks that I intend to keep my expense accounts down. It's going to be bad enough to have to get a new key from the locksmith. I looked all over for the key, but couldn't find it. Ask everybody I'd remembered was standing around this morning if they'd taken it. But nobody would admit to it. Damn! I just can't get Mort out of my mind. To think of him killing himself. I've been through his papers and letters, but couldn't dig out one reason. I've about come to the conclusion that maybe he learned he had an incurable ailment of some kind. I know he's acted worried lately."

"It's possible," Quist nodded carelessly. He said apropos of nothing in particular, "Nice place Guthrie has, out to the Bench-G."

"You were out there today?"

Quist nodded. "Trying to find out what he was doing in town so late last night—"

"I didn't know he was," Crawford said quickly.

"I didn't feel like attending the inquest, but I thought maybe I could help you some other way by trying to uncover someone who had talked to the sheriff. But I wasn't much help. Guthrie claimed he was trying to see Sheldon and Mort wouldn't allow it. So I didn't learn anything for you, Jeff."

"Danged nice of you to try, anyway, Greg. I'm going to need all the help I can get on this job. It sort of scares me."

"You'll get over that. Well, I've got to drift down to the station and see if the boss has sent any orders for me to move on. I never know from one day to the next where I'll be sent. I'll see you again, Jeff." Crawford nodded and Quist continued on his way.

At the station he found a single telegram from the Divisions Superintendent awaiting him: REQUEST BEING HONORED. JAY.

Quist went back to the hotel and up to his room, purposely delaying his supper until the dining room would be nearly empty. It worked out as he hoped and by the time he had about finished eating, Leila Monroe again joined him with her cup of coffee.

"I hope," Quist observed, "this is getting to be a regular habit and that I may look forward to it evenings."

Mrs. Monroe dimpled. "I'm frank in saying I enjoy someone new to talk to. Horcado City can be pretty boring at times. Unless there's some entertainment to attend, I have nothing but an empty house to face when I leave here."

"You don't have a room here in the hotel?"

Mrs. Monroe shook her head. "I rent a small place over on Atacosa Street, right next to Doctor Nash's house. The place is almost tiny—just a front room, bedroom and kitchen. Some time when we're better acquainted, I'd like to have you pay me a visit."

"I've nothing to do this evening," Quist said quickly.

"Oh, no, Mr. Quist, you can't work that fast," she laughed, and changed the subject. "I didn't see you at the inquest this afternoon."

"Did you go?" Quist looked surprised.

"I—and the rest of the town. What else is there to do here?"

"What did you think of it?"

"Oh, it turned out to be a show for people, I suppose. Really, it was rather horrible to think of Mort Beadle locking himself in and then using his own gun—" She broke off and took a sip of coffee. "I can't understand why he did it. I liked Mort, he had a lot of good points."

"You planned to marry him at one time, didn't you?"

Mrs. Monroe shook her head. "Mort had ideas in those directions, but I never gave him any encouragement. I just looked upon him as a good friend. He was always very gentlemanly, and I appreciated it."

"What sort of a sheriff do you think Jeff Crawford will make?"

She frowned. "I don't know,"—hesitatingly.

"What have you against Jeff?"

"Oh, not a thing," she said brightly. "Really, I haven't. I—well, it's just that—honestly I'd better not say any more. I've got to get out to the kitchen, Mr. Quist."

She acted a bit flurried and Quist didn't try to detain her. He watched her departing form, his eyes admiring. Then a frown gathered on his forehead. "Damned if she doesn't act like she's afraid of something. I wish I could persuade her to tell me something of Monroe's early life," he said to himself.

For the next two days, nothing happened, while Quist racked his mind to dovetail certain thoughts he'd worked out. The day after the inquest he'd attended Mort Beadle's funeral at the town Boot Hill, across the railroad tracks. There'd been a big turnout for the ceremonies with all the ranchers and men in the vicinity attending. Scott Fletcher rode down from Tourmaline, Leila Monroe was in a green corduroy riding costume which did more than merely enhance her beauty. She rode back to town with Quist later, but talked but little. Quist left the buckskin at the livery, along with her horse, then climbed the steps to the gallery where he dropped into a chair and sat glowering at passers-by.

"Lord, I've got a mind like a bowl of oatmeal," he muttered. "I know how the bastard did it, but what did he use? There was some way of relocking that office door—damn it, there has to be!"

That day passed and the next. The following day Quist was again seated on the gallery, no nearer to a solution to his problem than he had been previously. Impatiently, he strode down to the railroad depot to see if any telegrams had arrived. The stationmaster was on the platform directing the movement of a crate being pushed by a man in overalls on a small handtruck.

"Just take it right in the freight-shed, Bumpus," the stationmaster was saying. "Fritz will tell you where to place it. Let him do the worrying."

Bumpus was a short stocky man with a round face, in soiled blue overalls and a weather-beaten felt hat, the rim of which was torn and hung down over one ear. The stationmaster looked up and saw Quist, said goodday to him. Bumpus too put down his truck, and grinned widely, saluting Quist with a deferential touching of two fingers to the battered hat rim.

Quist nodded shortly and turned back to the station-master. The stationmaster was saying exasperatedly, "Keep going, Bumpus."

The man picked up his truck and disappeared within the freight-shed. "No, Mr. Quist, no wires for you today. You know, Mr. Quist, I always figured that Jay Fletcher wanted to save on expenses. He's always after us to cut down, and I do my best, but—"

"What's wrong?"

"That fellow with the handtruck. He arrived yesterday with orders from Jay Fletcher that he was to be put to work. Now we don't need any more help here.

I don't know what to do with him, except for odd jobs."

Quist shrugged. "Likely somebody Jay had to make a place for. Isn't he any good?"

"Oh, he tries. He's a good worker, all right. Acts like he has the care of the road on his shoulders. Always worrying for fear things won't run right, where to stack freight and so on. When he has nothing else to do he grabs a broom, spends half his time sweeping the platform and the station. He's already worn out one broom and I had to get him another one. The fact is, we just don't need him."

"I'll mention it to Jay at the first opportunity. What's his name?"

"Willie Bumpus. Imagine such a name. And I had to lend him a dollar when he arrived broke. He's sleeping in the freight-shed nights on an old blanket he brought with him."

"Don't let it bother you. Like's not he'll be transferred before long."

Quist sauntered slowly back to Trail Street, mind intent on his problem. "It's getting so I don't have anything to look forward to except that after-supper talk with Leila." By this time they'd reached the Greg and Leila stage, but Quist was making no further progress. "She's got something on her mind, but every time I try to pin her down she finds she has to run off to the kitchen."

He stopped at the corner of Deming and Trail Streets and moodily watched people pass. "Lord, if something would only break, so I'd get some action," he muttered. He considered for a moment getting his horse and riding up to Tourmaline, then discarded that notion. "I've nothing to tell him and if Sheila happened to be there I'd just be the fifth wheel on the wagon."

Thinking of Tourmaline, his mind recurred to the day he and Scott Fletcher had brought the wounded Tilford and Sheldon in for bandaging, before they were brought to town. "Which reminds me I never did get around to swearing out warrants against those two, or even questioning them. Not that that would do any good. They've had their mouths shut. Could be they're damn glad to stay in jail while they heal, for fear their mouths would get shut permanently. I'll have to talk to Doc Nash. Tilford's wound wasn't so much. With Scott jerking that slug out so soon—"

Quist's thoughts stopped suddenly. He wheeled about and strode swiftly in the direction of the sheriff's office, then slowed pace and lazed up the steps and across the porch. Jeff Crawford was working at the desk, a pile of papers in front of him. "Oh, hello, Greg. What's on your mind?"

"I suddenly remembered I hadn't sworn out those warrants against Tilford and Sheldon yet. Thought maybe you and I could—"

"Gosh, could you postpone it, Greg?" Crawford cut in. "The city council has asked that I get all Mort's papers and accounts in order and turn them over to them. Mort never did have much order in things like that, and it's a job sorting them out. They've sort of got me rushed. Maybe by tomorrow——"

"Sure, Jeff, sure. I'm in no hurry. I reckon Tilford and Sheldon will keep for a spell. I'll see you when you've more time."

Quist left the sheriff's office, noting as he did so that several of the Monroe hands were hanging around in front of the War-Drum, Vink Fisher among them. Swinging back the way he had come, Quist sauntered leisurely along Trail Street, until he reached Deming. Here he turned and quickened pace. At Atacosa he turned a second time, then slowed pace somewhat as he neared Crockett Street, scanning the houses on the north side.

"The northeast corner of Crockett and Atacosa," Quist mused. "Now, if Keg Hooper gave me the right information, that's the house."

He looked the house over as he approached. It was a large two-story structure painted brown, with a flight of steps ascending to the front door which stood closed. A bay window was on either side and in one of them was a sign reading "Roomers Taken," done in heavy black crayon and crude lettering.

"Most rooming houses leave their front doors unlocked during the day," Quist muttered. "Here's hoping I have luck."

He glanced both ways along the street. A block off, some children were playing in the roadway. In the other direction a pedestrian was just entering a house. Otherwise the street was empty. As though he had a

174

right to do so, Quist ascended the steps of the rooming house, tried the front door, found it unlocked and stepped inside.

Boldly Quist ascended the stairs, disregarding a creak in one step. There was a shorter hall above. There were two closed doors at the left and two at the front. What was it Keg Hooper had said? Oh, yes, one of the back rooms, but he wasn't certain which one. From behind one of the closed rear doors, Quist could hear a woman's soft voice.

He listened at the door opposite. There was nothing to be heard. He tried the knob. The door was locked. It was an old-fashioned type of lock, and Quist anticipated no difficulties. He drew out a bunch of keys of various sizes and types, selected one and tried it in the lock. It failed to budge the bolt. Quist tried another and another. His fourth effort succeeded, and an instant later he was in the room, closing the door softly behind him.

It was a typical room of its kind. Bed, still unmade, dresser, commode and one chair. Various articles of clothing hung on a stand. There was a window at the back, with the shade drawn halfway and some dingy-looking lace curtains. On the wall in an oak frame and glass was a steel engraving depicting "The Stag at Bay." Quickly, Quist ran his hands through the pockets of the clothing, but without success in his search. Next he turned his attentions to the drawers of dresser and commode. Quist opened them and found them empty, except for some cockroach occupants. Closed them again.

Cursing softly under his breath, Quist straightened and looked around. The picture on the wall caught his attention. He reached between picture frame and wall, fingers groping toward the nail which suspended the picture wire. Straddling the nail, over the wire that supported the frame, Quist found what he sought and drew it out. In one hand he now held the needle-nose pliers which Fletcher had said were missing the day he had extracted the bullet from Tilford's shoulder.

Quist slipped the pliers in his pocket, left the room, relocked it with the same key with which he'd entered, then moved softly down the stairway, passed through the hall, opened the door and made his way quickly to the sidewalk. A half block away he drew from his pocket the needle-nose pliers and the key to the sheriff's office. Clamping the jaws of the pliers down hard on the stem of the key, he looked eagerly for any mark they might have left on the surface. An exclamation of exultation left his lips. The mark cut into the stem was identical with the mark already existing on the rusted end of the pin. Things were beginning to clear up now.

XVIII

A couple of hours later he encountered Jeff Crawford on Trail Street. They stopped a minute on the sidewalk in front of Emmet & Ryan's General Store. "Get the job finished for the town council?" Quist asked.

Crawford nodded, indicating the paper-wrapped parcel he carried. "What a mess of records. Whew! I was just taking them in to Councilman Ryan. What he and the council will do with them, damned if I know. This job's wearing me out already. I sure wish Mort hadn't killed himself."

"He didn't," Quist said quietly. "He was murdered."

Crawford stiffened. "What in hell are you saying?" Quist repeated the words. "Oh, hell, Quist," Crawford continued, "I think you've got the wrong idea. Why, how could he have been killed? He locked himself in the office and—"

"That office was locked *from the outside,* after the murder."

"Don't see how it could be . . . look here, can you prove this?"

"I'll prove it when the time comes, Jeff. I won't say more now."

Crawford's face was a study in consternation. "Look here—uh—did you know this before the inquest?" Quist had suspected it, he said. "Damn it, you should have told me," Crawford complained.

"I wanted more evidence, Jeff, before I told anybody." He added, "I'm asking you to keep this under your hat until I'm ready to talk, sheriff."

Crawford forced a thin smile. "It doesn't seem right calling me 'sheriff.' I'll just have to get used to it, I guess. Oh, sure, I won't say a word, even if I think you're wrong. Let's talk it over some more when I've got more time, Greg."

"Suits me," Quist nodded and strolled off down the street.

Twenty minutes later, from his vantage point on the hotel gallery, he saw Jeff Crawford hurrying up Deming Street. "Bet he's headed for his rooming house," Quist chuckled. He waited for a time, then left the gallery and walked east on Trail Street to a pool room on the south side. Under the pretense of watching the players shoot pool, he saw through the window a half hour later, a number of the Monroe hands lounging about the front of the War-Drum Saloon. Webb Monroe came out once, then again re-entered the saloon. Crawford came hurrying down the street, a heavy frown on his face. He stopped a moment to talk to the Monroe hands, then hurried within the saloon.

"And so maybe I've started something," Quist mused. "We'll see what move they make next." Leaving the pool room, he headed back to the hotel and mounted the stairs to his room, expecting every minute to hear a knock on his door, but none came. The shadows deepened in the room. After a time he pulled down the shades and lighted the lamp. Six o'clock passed. Seven. Quist frowned. "It's sure taking them a hell of a time to make up their minds about what they'll do."

It was about eight o'clock when he descended the stairs and entered the dining room. Most of the diners had left by this time. Webb Monroe was just leaving. He nodded pleasantly but didn't stop for conversation.

Quist continued on in, found a table and gave his order.

Leila Monroe appeared with her cup of coffee while he was finishing his pie. There was something nervous in her manner, as she seated herself across from him, and Quist judged she'd been talking to her ex-husband. Perhaps they'd quarreled about something. She cast a quick glance around as Quist rose and placed a chair for her. The only other diners in the place got up to go. One of the waitresses was tidying up the tables. In a few minutes she too departed and Leila and Quist were alone in the room.

"These evening talks have meant a great deal to me, Greg," Leila was saying.

"I didn't think I was that important," Quist smiled.

She gave him a quick glance from beneath lowered lashes. *Lord, she's lovely,* he thought. "I've someone now to talk to," Leila went on. "I'm going to miss you when you leave. You're not married, are you, Greg?"

Quist shook his head, saying harshly, "A man in my job has no business marrying. I'm on the move too much."

"That's something I'm contemplating—moving."

"Why? You have a good position here and—"

"I know now I could get a similar position any place I went. I feel I've proved myself here. I want to leave. Greg—Greg—I'm frightened."

"Of what?"

"I don't dare tell you—now—" She moved in her chair.

Quist raised a protesting hand. "Now don't go running off to the kitchen like you usually do when I start asking things. What are you afraid of? Has your husband been making trouble?"

"Husband?" She glanced curiously at Quist. "Have you forgotten I'm divorced from Webb Monroe?"

"I've not forgotten you claim you were divorced, Leila," Quist said gently. "But you don't have to keep up that front with me. The records in Dallas have been checked and there is nothing to show—"

"Greg!" For a moment, indignation tinged her startled tones, then she seemed to slump, her eyes not meeting his. "All right," her words were muffled, "perhaps we never were married. God knows I've tried to keep it quiet, since Webb and I split up. You must be the only outsider who knows—"

"And I'm not planning to spill it alt over town." Quist said.

"You—you—" She glanced quickly up, the dark eyes moist. "I wonder now what you think of me?"

"No less than I ever did," Quist said promptly.

She reached across the table, touched his hand lightly, caressingly for a moment. "Greg, you're kind," she said, low-voiced. "And all I've ever heard was that you were ruthless, even cruel. I'll never believe it again. You're honest, good, and I—well, maybe I haven't always been on the level with you. Greg, did you miss a package from your room a few days back?"

Quist smiled. "Were you surprised when you opened the package, Leila?"

"I'd no idea what it contained. Someone else was surprised, surprised and in a rage. How did you know I took it?"

"It couldn't have been anyone else around here. I've talked to Merle Inwood. He'd questioned the girl who cleans my room. She couldn't have taken it. But you had the perfect opportunity. Who else would have a better chance to slip unnoticed, unsuspected, behind the desk and get the key to my room? Why did you want that old bow?"

She faced him directly now. "Yes, I did it—under force of threats. Why he wanted it, I don't know. I'm being honest with you now, Greg."

"Who wants the bow?"

Leila swallowed hard. "Greg, I don't dare tell you things here. I never know who may be watching me. I don't mind admitting I'm horribly frightened. Such terrible things have happened. First, Beriah Fletcher was killed—he was a good man, Greg. And now the sheriff has committed suicide."

"He was murdered," Quist said bluntly.

Her eyes widened, staring at him. "No, oh, no," she half-whispered. "No, that can't be true, Greg."

"I'm telling the truth, Leila."

She rose from her chair. "I've got to go now. They'll think it queer, out in the kitchen—" She was shaking her head in disbelief, an expression of fright and horror on her face.

Quist was on his feet, catching at her arm. "You've got to tell me what you know, Leila."

"No, Greg, no. I don't dare."

Quist still retained hold of her arm. "Tonight, Leila?"

"No. Please don't ask me. I'd be too afraid." Quist insisted, speaking fast, pointing out it was the sensible thing to do. She hesitated, then a trace of defiance entered her voice. "All right, Greg. I'll tell you everything you want to know. But not here. I'll be home by ten o'clock. Come then. My house is right next to Doctor Nash's, on Atacosa Street. I'll see you then."

XIX

He turned in past the trunk of the live oak and followed the path to the door. Here he paused a moment, then knocked. The door was opened immediately. Leila had been listening for his step. "Come in, Greg," she whispered breathlessly. "Hurry!"

She took his hat and placed it on a chair. He stood gazing at her, then her arms were lifting with his and he was holding her tightly to him, and feeling her heart racing madly against his breast, her moist lips seeking his. For a long moment, neither moved. A broken sob shook her trembling frame. "Oh, Greg, I've been so frightened but I feel safe when I'm in your arms." She was the first to move away. "We've got so much to talk about, Greg. I should have picked up a bottle and some cigars for you but I just didn't remember until I got home. I do have some coffee hot. I'll get it."

"That will be fine," Quist said.

He seated himself, back to bedroom, and accepted the cup of coffee she handed him. Idly he stirred in sugar and refused the tinned milk. She told him to smoke if he liked.

He could put his ashes on the tray. He rolled a cigarette and lighted it, and placed the burnt match carefully to one side, scarcely knowing how to begin. The coffee was hot and good, and Quist said so.

Finally she drew a long sigh and spoke reluctantly, "What is it you want to know, Greg?"

"I'd like to learn just how Monroe persuaded Mort Beadle to witness a forged bill-of-sale for Beriah Fletcher's Rafter-F."

"You knew it was a forgery?" she asked quickly.

"I couldn't figure anything else. Monroe looked crookeder than a dog's hind leg to me."

"You're right, Greg, you're so right." She shook her head. "From the time we came here he started stealing cows from both Mead Guthrie and Fletcher. He tried to make trouble between the two hoping to start a range war so he could clean them both out. I tried to talk him out of what he was doing but he just laughed at me." She paused. "I threatened to leave him. Webb said if I did he'd spill what he knew, and I didn't dare cross him—"

"What did Monroe have on you, Leila?"

"I'd rather not say, Greg. Some day I'll tell you. I was pretty young when it happened, but—oh, Greg, I can't go on. Some other time. Let's stick to the story.

Finally Webb said he had a plan to get the Rafter-F. He got a paper with Fletcher's signature, so he'd have something to copy on a forged bill-of-sale for the Fletcher holdings. He went there and paid Beriah Fletcher twenty-thousand dollars he'd got from Guthrie, and signed a paper promising to pay thirty thousand more every six months. This was all above-board and was witnessed by Mort Beadle. There were two copies made of the paper, and Webb and Fletcher each retained one. Webb and Fletcher were to meet at the bank in town and put the deal through in more legal fashion, with the signing of the deed and so on."

Quist took up the story. "But Monroe wanted to get back the paper saying he still owed thirty thousand, as well as the twenty thousand he'd paid. Is that right?" Leila nodded and Quist continued, "So that same night Monroe and his men raided the place in Tour-maline and killed Fletcher and stuck an arrow smeared with red paint in his back to make it look like the work of Indians. And after Fletcher was dead, Monroe forged a bill-of-sale stating he had paid to Fletcher fifty-thousand cash. And the court upheld Monroe's claim. Later, Monroe sold the Rafter-F to Guthrie."

"But he never did get the 'twenty-thousand dollar' paper back, or the money," Leila said, low-voiced. "Fletcher put up quite a fight and they had hard work breaking into his place. He must have guessed Webb would try something of the sort, and was ready for him. There was an Indian, called Nick, with Fletcher and from the amount of firing that was done, Webb and his men thought that the Indian was inside the house with Fletcher, but when they broke in the door, only Fletcher was there. They didn't know how the Indian got out. Later, one of the men saw Nick dodging through the brush and over the rocks near the house, and they took after him. The Indian gave them a long chase, but they finally caught up and killed him, too. They thought perhaps Nick had the money and that paper Webb wanted to get back, but they never found the paper or the money."

Quist looked a bit grim. "Mort Beadle had an honest name. How did Monroe ever persuade him to witness a forged signature on the 'fifty-thousand dollar' paper?"

"Sheriff Beadle had some gambling debts and Webb promised to take care of them for him if he'd sign as witness."

"I think there was more than that to it, Leila," Quist hinted.

Leila averted her eyes. Then she looked at him directly. A hopeless tone entered her voice. "You're right and I'm afraid you're going to hate me, Greg, but I must tell the truth. I'd already left Webb and come to town. Webb asked me to be nice to Mort Beadle and persuade him to come into the deal. Mort thought I was in love with him and—and—well after Fletcher was dead, Mort didn't want his doings made public. He consented."

"And you threw him over later," Quist said harshly. "You didn't want your part of it made public either, so from then on you were nice to anybody Webb told you to be nice to." The girl didn't say anything, but touched a handkerchief to her eyes. Quist said bitterly, "Webb Monroe should be—" He broke off, "What's Jeff Crawford's part in this deal?"

"Crawford is really on Webb's payroll, has been from the start, when he brought him here. He persuaded Mort to appoint him deputy, so he could keep an eye on Mort. Webb said that Mort was always having an attack of conscience and he was afraid that Mort might confess some day to the authorities. Jeff Crawford was to keep an eye on him, keep him in line, as Webb said."

"And you kept an eye on Crawford," Quist charged. Leila said weakly, "Jeff sometimes called on Sheila Guthrie, when her father would let him."

"I've a hunch," Quist said shortly, "that that was just a cover so people wouldn't notice his interest in you." Leila didn't say anything but bowed her head. "And after his father was killed and Scott Fletcher came back, I suppose it was Monroe who arranged to get two cowhands on Guthrie's crew and have them kill Scott, thus throwing more blame in Guthrie's direction. But that didn't work. You played up to Guthrie too for a time, didn't you?"

Leila brushed the back of her hand across her long lashes but faced Quist squarely. "All right, it's so. Think what you like of me, Greg. I know what I've been—and I know now I'm frightened."

"You mean you know too much and you fear

Monroe will have you killed, as he had Mort Beadle murdered?"

"You haven't missed much, have you, Greg?"

"I know it was murder and how Crawford did it. Leila, if you want me to be honest with you, you've got to come clean with me. What do Monroe and his gang expect me to do?"

"Greg, you've got to believe me. I've had to do what Webb demanded, even after I left him, but it hasn't been easy. You must understand or things will never be the same between us again. I've feared for my life for years now—"

"I asked you a question, Leila. What does Monroe think I know?"

"He's not sure. He just fears you. He's always been afraid that the 'twenty-thousand dollar' paper will show up, and knock all his scheming sky-high. Then when you showed up with that old bow you'd found with the skeleton that bothered him and he wanted to get hold of the bow, fearing you must have had some reason for hanging on to it the way you did. He thought Scott Fletcher had hired you to come here. When his men killed that Indian, Nick, they'd seen the bow but left it there, thinking nothing of it. When you brought the bow to town, Webb figured perhaps some sort of message had been written on it."

"Message?"

"Words stating where the paper and the money had been put. And when he couldn't get the bow he was nearly frantic. Your refusals drove him crazy. Then he told me to steal it from your room."

Quist smiled. "What he got drove him still crazier, I reckon."

"He was terribly unpleasant, Greg."

"You've been mighty frank, Leila." Quist took a sip of coffee.

"Greg," she asked curiously. "What did you do with that old bow? Hid it, I suppose. But where? And what did you learn from it?"

"Not a solitary single thing, Leila," he laughed, gathering his legs beneath him. "I know no more of it now than I ever did. I'd hoped you could throw some light on the mystery."

"Really, Greg?" A tinge of angry color flooded her features.

"Really." Now, why was she angry? Unless. . . . *Here it comes.* . . .

He rose suddenly, kicking the chair back of him, springing to the center of the room just as Vink Fisher burst from behind the bedroom curtain, six-shooter already blazing. Quist heard Leila's shrill scream as the table went over. A slug whined past him, but he was moving too fast to make a good target.

Three times Quist's underarm .44 jumped in his fist, the heavy detonations blending with the explosions of Fisher's weapon. Fisher stiffened in midstride then, whirled off balance by the tremendous impact of Quist's shots, crashed against a chair and went down, his gun clattering from his grasp.

Powdersmoke swirled through the room. Quist glanced quickly around. Both Leila and Fisher lay without movement. The lamp lay on its side, chimney and globe shattered, oil leaking from the base. A moment more and the jumping flame from the wick would catch. Quist stooped quickly, righted the lamp and then the table. He set the chimneyless, globeless lamp on the table, where it made a torch to light the grim scene.

Fisher lay on his back, crimson seeping into his shirt-front. There was no doubt about him. Quist crossed over and knelt at Leila's side, feeling for her pulse. There wasn't any. He'd moved too fast away from the table and the first bullet from Fisher's gun had missed him and struck Leila Monroe.

Methodically, Quist plugged out the empty shells in his gun and reloaded, replacing the gun in holster. Yells were heard along the street and the sound of windows being flung open. Quist again cast a look at Leila. "I'll say one thing for you, lady, you were true to Webb Monroe—right up to the last."

Steps pounded on the path leading to the house. Quist opened the door. "You got here unusually fast, Sheriff Crawford," he said.

Anger twisted Crawford's features. "My God, what's happened here? Leila! And Vink Fisher!" For a moment he couldn't speak. The door was still open and Doctor Nash came bounding in. "Did I hear shots—?" He broke off, momentarily speechless at the scene before him. Other men were crowding the

189

doorway now. Quist shut the door, and turned back to the room, picking up his sombrero from a chair. Crawford and Nash were both shooting questions at him.

"There's not much to tell," Quist said wearily. "Mrs. Monroe invited me for a cup of coffee. While we were talking, Vink Fisher came bursting from behind that curtain. My gun happened to be faster than his. His first shot missed me and struck Mrs. Monroe."

Nash knelt at Leila's side. He rose after a moment and went to examine Fisher. "Too late for me to do anything," he stated.

"Look here, Quist, I don't like this—" Crawford started.

"That makes two of us," Quist said.

"But what proof have we it was Fisher who shot Leila?"

Quist said, "Fisher carries a forty-five. I use a forty-four. When the doctor's probed out the slugs you'll see what I mean. Only Fisher was killed with forty-fours. That good enough for you, Jeff?"

Crawford frowned. "But why should Fisher attack you?"

"If you put it that way, why should I attack him? I had nothing to fear from him until he started this mix-up. I'd say, who paid Fisher to attack me?"

"What do you mean by that?"

"Think it over, Jeff. And let me know what decision you reach."

"Look here, Greg, I hate to do it, but I feel I must place you under arrest."

"Don't let your new authority go to your head,

sheriff," Quist snorted scornfully. "And don't try to arrest me. I'll bust you wide open if you do."

Doctor Nash interrupted. "Don't talk fool talk, Jeff. If Mr. Quist says he didn't shoot Mrs. Monroe, I'm willing to take his word for it. As he says, the autopsy has a story to tell."

"All right, when can we have it?" Crawford snapped. "We should have an inquest tomorrow—"

"T'hell we should," Nash said testily. "I'm expecting a delivery tomorrow morning. Then I'll have two autopsies to go through with. We'll set that inquest, for both Mrs. Monroe and Fisher, for day after tomorrow."

"You two settle it between you," Quist cut in. "I'm going to bed."

"You'll be around when you're needed?" Crawford demanded.

"I'll be around," Quist snapped. He nodded to the doctor, turned and strode from the house. Crawford stared after him, not daring to protest further, his features livid with angry frustration.

XX

". . . and so that's the story," Quist was saying. "It was a rigged plot to finish me, after Leila had done some pumping. I could have grabbed both Crawford and Monroe, Scott, but I might have been downed in the attempt, and I thought I'd better let you have the facts first. Besides I figured you deserved to be in at the finish."

He sat talking to Sheila Guthrie and Scott Fletcher in Fletcher's house, after having spent most of the day in Horcado City waiting for Crawford and Monroe to take action of some sort; rather than wait longer and face continual questions regarding the previous night's killings, he had saddled up the buckskin and rode to Tourmaline where he had found Scott and Sheila engaged in archery practice. That had stopped when he drew them into the house and told his story.

"Good Lord, Greg," Scott exclaimed. "You must have steel nerves. I don't see how you could sit there all that while, with your back to that curtain, knowing someone was waiting to plug you."

"It wasn't any fun," Quist admitted. "Every so often Fisher gave himself away by breathing too heavily, or shifting a foot. Likely he felt right tense too. But I gambled he wouldn't shoot until I'd spilled everything about the bow." Quist reached into his pocket and produced a pair of needle-nosed pliers which he handed to Scott. Scott looked surprised. Quist explained, "The pliers you couldn't find the other day, Scott. Crawford must have had it in mind to kill Beadle for some time. These pliers were just what he needed. I figure he came in here, after you and I rode up to look at that skeleton, and searched for the bow, before telling Tilford and Sheldon to go ahead and drop us—"

"But how, exactly—?" Scott started.

"It was simple enough," Quist explained. "Crawford let himself into the sheriff's office after Beadle was asleep, then knocked him on the head. Taking time to split the end of one of Beadle's ca'tridges, he next shot the sheriff. That done, he left the office, closed the door, and inserting these pliers into the outside key-hole, turned the key and locked the door. It looked foolproof—to him."

Sheila said suddenly. "Scott, when this comes out, the case will go to court again. Dad won't have clear title to the Bench-G. It will be your property if—"

"We'll worry about that when the time comes," Scott said.

The girl turned to Quist. "Dad must know what is in the wind. I've never seen him more depressed than he's been since you visited us. He didn't even reopen the matter of me seeing Scott against his wishes."

"What's the next move, Greg?" Scott asked.

"I've given that a mite of thought. Monroe's men when they tracked down Nick and killed him, couldn't understand how he had gotten out of the house. I think your Dad had Nick leave by the trapdoor when the attack came. He hoped that Nick would not be noticed. The quiver was left behind for reasons of stealth. It was just Nick's bad luck to get caught. Your Dad wouldn't have sent him off, unless he'd given Nick something to implicate Monroe."

"But so far as we know, all Nick had was his bow."

"Well, Monroe had an idea the bow has some sort of message written on it. He was bothered to hell when I wouldn't let him have it. That increased his fears. So maybe we've overlooked something. What do you think?"

Scott shook his head. "I examined that bow right careful."

"Did you look beneath the rawhide wrapping on the handle?"

Scott's jaw dropped. "No! I didn't. I remember noticing the rawhide wasn't wound as neatly as most of Dad's jobs. It looked hurried. Just a sec and we'll give a look."

The table was dragged beneath the trapdoor and a chair placed on it. Scott climbed up and lifted the door. A moment later he had reclosed it and handed the wrapped bow to Quist. Sheila looked on, wide-eyed. The table and chair were replaced. With hands that shook slightly, Scott unwrapped the tarpaulin and exposed the old osage bow to light. The rawhide strips were loosened and unwound. The two men scrutinized the handle and riser, now bare to their vision. "I just don't see—" Scott began dubiously. Then, "Look! This is the neatest job Dad ever turned out."

"In what way?" Quist looked puzzled.

"Instead of gluing the riser to the bow proper to make the handle," Scott said excitedly, "Dad made it inset, grooved and rabbeted, so the riser could be slid off—you know, like the sliding cover on a box. Here's a tiny hardwood plug at one end to hold it firmly in place, before the rawhide strips are wound on to hide the difference from regular bow handles. Now, we draw out this little plug and the riser slides off—so—" as he removed the riser sections of the handle. "Why, this riser is hollowed out, there's a small space—"

Scott looked excitedly at Quist and Sheila. "Now I know what Dad meant when he told Nick he'd not need a medicine bag for his knickknacks any more—though I guess Nick still wore that medicine bag—"

"There's something inside that riser," Quist said. "Take a look."

It was necessary to pry out the contents with Scott's knife-blade. First came a dried set of snake's rattles, which fell to the floor almost unnoticed, except for an excited "Wow!" from Sheila. Then Scott pried out a tightly folded paper with somewhat faded writing on it. Scott straightened out the paper. His gaze widened. "This is it!" he exclaimed. "Look, Greg, Sheila! Here's Monroe's signature promising to pay thirty-thousand dollars to Dad, spread over six-month payment intervals. It states clearly here that Dad received only twenty thousand, instead of the whole fifty that Monroe claimed was paid. Oh, this will sure cook Monroe's goose—"

"But where's the twenty thousand?" Quist put in. "Nick wasn't carrying it when he was caught, according to Leila Monroe—"

"Look here," Scott pointed out. "This is Dad's writing in lead pencil. From the words 'Twenty thousand' in ink, he's run a line to the edge, and there it says, *Try the wall. B.F.*"

"Try the wall?" Scott looked puzzled. "What does he mean?" He put down the bow and stared at Quist and Sheila.

"I've a hunch that your dad expected Monroe to try to get that money back," Quist stated. "Let me see, how thick are these walls here?"

"You mean he buried it in the wall? But where?" Scott gazed vacantly around the room.

"Where it wouldn't be seen right away," Quist said. "Let's try the wall behind the benches."

"Make it that sidewall bench. That front wall bench I put up when I came here."

The three of them went to work on the heavy workbench, dragging it away from the wall. Tools and archery equipment fell unnoticed to the floor. Finally they had the bench to the center of the room, and all eyes turned on the wall, composed of granite blocks of irregular size. Quist was first to spot a probability.

"Look here, see? This spot looks different from the rest of the wall. It's just dried mud holding the rock in place"—running his fingernail around the edge of the granite— "instead of cement like the rest. Got a chisel and hammer?"

The tools were quickly produced, and Quist got to work. It took but a few blows to show that the face of the rock was only a one-inch veneer. Behind was a small hollow chamber. Quist reached in and drew out a tin japanned box. It was unlocked. He threw back the cover. "There you are," he announced triumphantly.

The box was crammed with money—gold and bills of various denominations. On top lay a lead-penciled note:

Webb Monroe may come here tonight and try to get this money, so I take these precautions. Nick is a witness to what I've done, and if Monroe and his gang come later, Nick will slip away to bring help.
Beriah Fletcher.

No one spoke for a moment. Then Scott, his voice unsteady, "A right canny old codger, my dad. He knew if anything happened, I'd look up Nick right away. Only Nick never made it either. It's no wonder I never could find him."

The money was counted and proved out to be twenty thousand to the last dollar. Quist said, "I think, Scott, we'd best ride to town and put that money in the hotel safe until the bank opens in the morning. Then with the proof we have we'll move to apprehend Monroe, Crawford and the rest of the scuts. No, Sheila, you'd better not come with us. No telling what will happen when we hit town. You fork your pony and tell your father what we've learned."

"Greg's right, Sheila," Scott nodded. "We'll get started just as soon as we can saddle up—"

He broke off, listening. Approaching hoofbeats and the squeaking of saddle leather were heard. Quist strode to the door and flung it open. So intent had they been on their discoveries that the riders nearing the house had gone unnoticed.

Some twelve or fifteen horses came sweeping into the turn that led to Tourmaline's single street. Jeff Crawford was leading and just behind him was Webb

Monroe. Quist recognized several more of Monroe's hands. The faces of all were set in hard angry lines.

Quist snapped, "Scott, get Sheila back out of range. I don't like the looks of this."

The horsemen came plunging up. Jeff Crawford spied Quist as they stopped in a scattering of dust-clouds and scattered gravel.

"You, Quist," he yelled. "I'm putting you under arrest!"

"On what charge?" Quist calmly demanded.

"The murders of Leila Monroe and Vink Fisher. As an accomplice we're taking in Scott Fletcher too. Don't try to resist—"

Without finishing the words he reached for his gun. Quist's forty-four emerged in one swift movement, seeming to leap to meet his fist, and a stream of white fire spurted from the muzzle, as a slug ripped into the doorjamb at his side. Crawford swayed in the saddle and pitched to the earth, a long agonized cry torn from his lips.

Quist leaped within the house, slamming the door. "Now we're in for it!" he snapped. "Scott—"

The words were lost in the hail of lead that struck the front of the house, bullets flattening against the granite walls and shattering panes of glass in the windows.

"Blast 'em out of there!" came Webb Monroe's angry yell.

XXI

Quist went to one of the windows where a pane was missing and sent two shots flashing toward the milling riders. Scott was lifting into place the two heavy oaken bars that crossed the door, top and bottom. More windows crashed, the fusillade of outside firing increased, but no harm was done. Quist was fumbling in his pocket for cartridges and reloading. "That last shot of mine made them draw off," he stated grimly. "They're making plans for the next move probably—"

He broke off to help Scott and Sheila shove one of the heavy workbenches, lifted to one end, against the window. "Now the other bench at the other window," Scott panted. To Quist's surprise, Scott flung up the lower sash of the window before moving the upright bench against the opening. "Leave me about a six-inch slit there," Scott said. "I'll need an opening."

"What's the idea?" Quist asked.

"I said I'd never again use a gun, but if I draw a bead with an arrow, those scuts are going to know it," Scott snapped. "Now, let's fix the other window the same way."

It was quickly done; now the windows were effectually barred with the heavy hardwood benches, and both Quist and Scott had openings through which to fire. Scott had already chosen a bow and a supply of broadhead arrows.

"What can I do?" Sheila asked. She was pale but keeping her chin up.

"Just keep down and out of bullet range," Quist said. Scott nodded agreement, while he and Quist watched at the narrow openings.

"Here they come!" Quist snapped.

The riders came tearing toward the house, yelling like wild Apaches, their shots flattening against the granite wall and thudding into the door and workbenches. Quist fired two swift shots and saw a man pitch from his saddle. Then he heard the swift twang! twang! twang! of Scott's bow string. Even while he watched, gun poised, Quist saw an arrow take one of the riders directly beneath the breastbone. The man threw up his arms and toppled from his pony's back.

"Three cheers for Agincourt!" Quist yelled. "Nice shooting, Scott. They're retreating again."

It was true. Two men lay prone in the roadway, and a third was running as fast as he could, holding one leg from which an arrow was protruding. Within a few minutes all the riders had disappeared beyond the oak trees.

"They sure wasted a lot of lead without doing any damage," Quist observed, peering out.

"They'll never get us charging in like that," Scott said. "These granite walls will stand forever. I built that door myself, so I know it will stop a lot of slugs. These two workbenches will catch the devil I suppose, but they'll stand up."

"We're safe for the time being," Quist said. "What worried me is I only put a few ca'tridges in my pocket before I left. I'm running low on loads."

"Sheila," Scott said, "take a look in that cabinet at the back wall. Dad's old gun is there and there may be some ca'tridges for it. He used a forty-four."

Sheila announced after a moment, "Yes, there's a box of forty-fours here and another box of forty-fives. And two guns."

"The other six-shooter is mine," Scott said.

"Why can't I use the forty-five?" Sheila asked. "I'm not much of a shot, but—"

"You keep away from these windows," Scott commanded.

"But I feel so useless."

"Find some kindling. Start a small fire and boil a pot of coffee. There's some cold beef and bread in the cooler, too. Maybe we can stand a snack. It's getting 'long toward supper time. Look, here comes Brose Daulton with both hands in the air and he's waving a bandanna." They watched the man approach. Daulton shouted something. Scott said, "He's asking for a parley."

Quist peered through his opening and raised his voice. "Stop right where you are, Daulton. What do you want?"

"Webb warns you, you'd best surrender. We'll take you in to town for a fair trial, you and Fletcher. We won't hold the girl. You haven't got a chance, Quist. We were all legally swore in as a posse by Crawford,

201

so you'd better give up. It'll be the worse for you if you don't."

"It's no good, Daulton," Quist called back. "We couldn't be in a better position, so bring on your lead-slingers." Daulton tried to talk more, but Quist cut him short. "Get moving, Daulton, and join the rest of the rattlers." The man moved off, voicing threats.

"Could they starve us out?" Sheila asked, even-toned.

"They probably figure to do just that," Quist said. "Just keep your nerve up. Some how, some way, we'll get out of this jam yet."

Scott said, "Do you suppose we could sneak past them, Greg?"

"I doubt it. They'll be on watch for that sort of business. We'd have no chance without our horses, and once afoot they'd soon run us down. If Nick couldn't sneak past them, I doubt whether we could."

"I've a hunch they won't try another attack while the moon is high."

An hour passed while the moon swung slowly overhead. Suddenly Quist caught the sound of chopping. "Looks like they need some more wood for their fire," Scott said. "Some of 'em must have been sneaking along the backs of the houses across the street and found an old axe in one of those broken-down buildings."

"Could they be chopping down a tree to make a battering ram?" Sheila asked.

"Smart girl," Quist said. "I was just wondering the same thing."

The chopping noises went on for a time and then stopped. The hours dragged along. "That moon will be gone by midnight," Scott observed from his window. "Clouds gathering. Might even be a storm brewing up."

"Scott," Quist asked, "how far can you shoot an arrow?"

"Depends on the sort of arrow and the bow used. And how big a target you wanted to hit."

"I was thinking of a pretty large target. Say, the railroad tracks the other side of this shoulder of mountain we're trapped on. I believe you said it was about a quarter of a mile to the tracks, not counting the drop from the top of the shoulder."

"Yes, I could do it with a flight bow, Greg. What you aiming at?"

"Could you drop one of those steel broadhead arrows between the tracks, or near them, so the point would stick in the ground with the feather-end up?"

"It would naturally land that way, in an upright positon, unless it struck a stone to knock it sidewise—"

"So you'd have to shoot a number of arrows—"

"And I'd be shooting blind, you understand. From here I'd already have the height; it would be no job lifting an arrow over the top of the shoulder and it should drop easily down to the tracks. And the way that wind whips continually around the shoulder it should help hold the arrow down to where we want it, or drive it in the direction of Horcado City, along the tracks—but what you got in mind?"

"It occurred to me that the number four eastbound freight reaches Horcado City shortly after sun-up."

"And you think if the engineer saw an arrow sticking in the earth alongside the rails, he'd stop the train to pick it up? I doubt it. And how would that help us?"

"He'd stop the train to get the arrow if it had a red flag attached. I've yet to see the engineer who would knowingly run a red signal."

"Now, wait a minute, Greg. I've no red flags here. Even if I had I'm not sure the idea would work out—the weight of the flag—hell, I'd have to use my heaviest broadheads to offset that. You couldn't count on the flight, either. With a flag on it, the arrow would zig-zag or swerve crazily. The feathers couldn't hold it true. Anyway, I haven't any red flags."

"You've got red paint here. Haven't you any white cloth we could use?"

Scott pondered. "I've got a white dress-up shirt, but—"

Sheila cut in, "Scott! It's worth trying. As for white cloth, wait until I step out of this petticoat. It's white cambric." Quist caught the rustling of skirts, then, "Greg, how large a piece do you want for the flag—" Fletcher interrupted:

"I'll want about a dozen pieces." Scott's interest was picking up now. "Wait, I've got scissors some place around here that I trim feathers with. Make 'em small, like little pennants." He was already fumbling among his tools in the darkness.

"Throw up some sort of blind and light the lamp," Quist suggested. "You can't work in the dark. I'll keep watch here. Cut the pennants triangular, long enough to be spotted easy, but not so long they'll throw the arrow off flight."

"Easy for you to say," Scott said. "Harder to do." He placed a chair atop the table and threw blankets over it for a blind, then lighted the lamp and set it on the floor, but kept it turned low. He and Sheila started cutting out small pennants.

From the window where he stood watch, Quist spoke over his shoulder: "On the wide end of the pennant, use a heavy lead-pencil, or something you can write with. Just write, *'Help. Tourmaline. Quist.'* Leave enough space so the message can be read easily, then paint the rest of the pennant red."

From his window he scanned the street. There was no one in sight, but he could still hear sounds of chopping, and speculated that the outlaws were cleaning branches from their battering ram. Behind him, by the dim light from the lamp, Sheila and Scott worked steadily. Quist again glanced at the sky. Clouds were gathering swiftly and the light from the moon was almost obscured.

Sheila was busy printing the message at the wide end of the pointed pennants. After a time there came the noise of a light tapping. Scott said, "Greg, I'm using small staples to fasten these flags to the arrow shafts. Then they can be rolled tightly just before I shoot. Lord only knows what will happen when these pennants pass the bow. The arrows may fly every which way as the cloth comes loose."

"The red paint should prove sticky enough to hold them tight until they're well on their way," Quist offered. "Once they've landed, point down, in the ground, the wind whipping around the mountain shoulder should quickly unwind them, set them flying."

"That's an idea too," Scott answered. He came through the gloom to the window. "Can you see this?" —holding out an arrow with a white pennant attached. "I've fastened it back by the feathers. Rolled tightly, the bulk may not affect my release too much."

There was still enough light from the waning moon for Quist to read the message Sheila had printed: *Help. Tourmaline. Quist.* Quist said, "Lord that's a heavy broadhead."

"Biggest I have. Guaranteed to stop a grizzly if it strikes right. I'm going to need that weight. Shooting about a dozen arrows, using a special flight bow."

"What's special about it?"

"Shorter than a target or hunting bow, but much wider. I'll go up on the roof to release these pennant-arrows, strap the bow to my feet, with my legs elevated, lay on my back and fire away, hoping for the best—"

"You joshing me, Scott?"

"Not at all, Greg. I'll need the strength of both arms to draw back the arrow and bow string, on a bow of such poundage. It hits close to two hundred pounds.

With my legs elevated I'll get the proper angle for the distance. Seen anything of the Monroe gang—?"

"Not a sign. I can hear them from time to time. I figure they're waiting until it gets darker, when we can't aim so well. They've maybe learned to fear your arrows."

"And your gun." Scott went back to rejoin Sheila and Quist saw them busy with red paint. The time had passed so swiftly that it was already past midnight. Half an hour later, the moon was completely gone. Once Quist fired at what he took to be a man moving on hands and knees along the street, but finally decided he had been wasting his shot on a clump of sage moving in the breeze.

It must have been around one-thirty when Quist caught the sound of Scott's grunting as he worked to string the heavy flight bow. Sheila said something about having red paint on her hands, and Scott told her where she could find a tin of turpentine. The light was blown out within a few minutes and Scott moved table and chair beneath the trapdoor. "I'm going above, Greg," he called.

"Good luck, Scott."

"We're going to need all the luck we can get," Scott returned as his legs disappeared through the square opening in the ceiling. Sheila was on the table now, handing up his equipment. Then footsteps scraped on the roof. . . . Quist hoped he was staying low, though with the darkness there was slight chance of any Monroe man seeing him.

Sooner than Quist had expected, Scott was back and the trapdoor reclosed. Sheila said, "How'd it go, Scott?" as they replaced the chair and table. "It was too dark to tell much," he admitted, "so I'm not sure. I released the arrows okay, but Lord knows where they went later. I thought I heard one strike a rock at the top of the shoulder, and maybe they all went haywire. We'll just have to hope for the best."

He again took up his position at the other window and had nothing to say when Quist told him all was quiet. About three in the morning Sheila provided beef and bread and cold coffee. Water was divided sparingly among the three. The sky was beginning to lighten in the east when Quist next spoke, "I hear a lot of activity at the Monroe camp. Maybe we'd best gird our loins for more trouble."

The sun was just rising above the eastern horizon when six men staggered into view, carrying with the aid of their throw-ropes, a huge tree trunk. "Here comes the battering ram," Quist said. "Hold your fire until they come closer."

Scott was fitting the nock of an arrow to his bow. "I'll have to wait," he said coolly, "until they reach an angle I can reach with an arrow. They're too far to one side for me to hit 'em through this narrow opening."

The men came on, behind them more men, guns at ready. A slug ripped into the bench shielding Quist. Lead began to strike the granite wall of the house and tear into the oaken door. The shooting reached a crescendo. Neither Quist nor Scott dared go near their openings. Greg called to Sheila: "Load those other two guns for me and keep them coming. The instant their firing lessens a minute, I'm going to cut loose."

The fire slackened off a moment while the battering-ram bearers squared off to face the door.

"Now!" Quist snapped, starting to fan slugs from his .44. He emptied his gun and felt another thrust into his hand by the girl. This too was emptied. He heard an almost continual *twanging* of Scott's bow string. Smoke swirled in the street.

Two men were down. Three more limping away. The rest running out of line of gun- and arrow-fire. The battering ram had been dropped to the middle of the street when the firing started. Monroe's angry cursing could be heard as he ordered his men back into the fight.

They returned half-heartedly to the fracas, none of them wanting to come within Quist's and Fletcher's range. For some time a steady hail of slugs battered against the front wall of the house, none of them doing any damage. Once a slug whined through the opening near Quist, narrowly missing his head, and flattened itself against the back wall.

Gradually the Monroe men withdrew and the shooting stopped. "They must have decided to figure out another plan," Quist said grimly. Burnt-powder stench stung eyes and throat and nostrils. There was a smear of grime across his forehead. He glanced at Scott, saw a splash of red on one hand. "You're hit, Scott!"

"Red paint." Scott grinned tiredly. Sheila again

brought around small portions of water and the men drank thirstily. The sun rose higher. Scott said, "I wonder if the train stopped. Sometimes you can hear it pass from up here, but there was so much shooting I didn't remember to listen."

Another hour passed. Off to one side, out of gun range, Monroe raised his voice. "You'd better give up, Quist. We'll make a deal with you. We'll leave Fletcher and the girl if you'll surrender."

Scott said savagely, "It's no good, Greg. If you give up, I will too—"

"And I!" Sheila snapped promptly.

Quist raised his voice. "Monroe, we need more time to talk things over and decide—"

"I'll give you one hour, Quist," Monroe's voice came back. "And no more. And I promise a fair trial for you."

Quist smiled at Scott and the girl. "I'd never reach town for a trial. And neither would you two get free. Anyway, there's an hour of grace we bargained for. We can take it easy for a spell—though I wouldn't trust to Monroe's word."

The sun lifted higher and long slanting shadows were cast across Tourmaline's single street. Quist glanced at his watch. "Cripes, it's eight-thirty. My hour must be nearly up." Already the sun's heat was seeping through the roof. There'd be no storm today. The clouds had all disappeared. Quist found himself wishing for a drink of water and knew the others felt the same.

More time passed before Monroe's voice was again heard, from off to one side. "Quist, what's your decision? You coming out?"

Quist called back, "I'm staying here, Monroe. It's too hot out in that sun."

Monroe cursed angrily. "Better think twice, Quist. We can blast that building out from under you."

"Blast away, scut, and see if you get any farther than you did with your other blastings."

"All right, you asked for it." Monroe laughed harshly and bawled to his men. "Come on, you hombres! Bring up the dynamite! We'll show Quist and his friends what blasting means."

Wild yells of fiendish glee arose from the Monroe men.

Quist exclaimed, "Dynamite! Where in the devil—?"

Something like a groan escaped Scott's lips. "They must have found the dynamite that prospector left in the old shack down the street. I knew I should have taken care of that long ago. They can plant it at the side of this place where we can't reach them with our shots. Oh, Lord, why did I—?"

"We're not licked yet," Quist cut in grimly. "If you and Sheila will cover me, I'll dash out and drop whoever tries to set the dynamite. There likely won't be more than three—no, Sheila has to stay inside. Scott, you—" He broke off, listening.

Sudden gunfire had broken out beyond the live oak trees. There were wild yells and the drumming of horse's hoofs. A man came fleeing past Quist's line of vision. Quist's .44 barked and the man went sprawling to the dust. There was more yelling and shooting.

Quist snapped, "What the devil—"

The firing was already dying down. A voice yelled, "Quist! Greg Quist! Where are you?"

"By God! That's Willie Bumpus! Coming, John!" he bawled.

He talked swiftly while he was removing the two heavy oaken bars from the door. "I sent word for extra authority—"

The words went unfinished as he seized his gun and went sprinting from the open doorway. By this time only sporadic shooting was heard. Quist dashed to the end of the street, swung around the clumps of live oaks and massive granite blocks, then stopped.

Some twenty men in saddles were rounding up the frantic Monroe crew. At one side, Webb Monroe was on the earth, hands raised begging for mercy. Jeff Crawford was down. He looked dead. Mead Guthrie's heavy voice was shouting orders. Men were swinging ropes, lashing Monroe hands, herding them into a small circle. A number of bodies were sprawled here and there.

Willie Bumpus, still in overalls and tattered hat brim, pushed up to meet Quist, a wide grin on his face. "You all right, Greg?" The men's hands went out to each other.

Sheila and Scott came running up to hear Bumpus telling Quist: "Of course we got your messages. The engineer of number four couldn't imagine what those red flags were flying for. Stuck on arrows, by Gawd, all along the right of way. He read what they said and pushed on for the station. The stationmaster started to take them, when I grabbed 'em from his hand. Then I started to rouse folks, men that hadn't ridden or fired a gun in years, but I got 'em going. We nearly killed the horses getting here. Luckily, Mead Guthrie and some of his men were in town—"

Quist interrupted, "Sheila—Scott—meet John Engle, alias Willie Bumpus. John and I have worked together, before, when I needed the authority of his Deputy U.S. Marshal's badge." He swung around as Mead Guthrie approached. "How come you were so handy, Mead?"

"I've done a lot of thinking since you talked to me the other day," Guthrie explained. "Yesterday, a Monroe rider came to the Bench-G, and when he left, half of my hands went with him. I can see now they never were really my hands. I kept thinking about that all evenin'. Then Sheila didn't come home. It hit me sudden that Monroe might be up to something. Finally about one, this morning, I roused all my hands and we took out for town—"

A cowhand cut in, "Monroe says he wants to make a confession."

"He'll have plenty of time," Quist said. "Go on, Mead."

"Couldn't locate Monroe or Sheriff Crawford in town. The sheriff's office was dark. We busted in, got the jail keys and started to question Sheldon and Tilford. It was nigh sun-up before we broke 'em down, and they admitted to Crawford having told them to dry-gulch you and Fletcher. Beyond that, all they claimed to know was that Crawford had raised a posse of Monroe hands to go to Tourmaline and arrest you fellers. Couldn't believe it at first, so I went down to the station to see if the stationmaster knew anything about you. 'Bout that time, the freight train rolled in, with the engineer talking excitedly about some red flags stuck on arrows along the tracks, with messages on 'em. From then on, Deputy U.S. Marshal Engle took over and we headed for here—and you know the rest. I can't figure where those arrows come from, less'n Scott Fletcher's responsible—"

"He was—tell Dad, Scott," Sheila laughed.

"Let's tell it in town over a couple of pitchers of ice-cold beer."

"I'm game," said Quist.

Center Point Publishing

600 Brooks Road ● PO Box 1
Thorndike ME 04986-0001 USA

(207) 568-3717

US & Canada:
1 800 929-9108
www.centerpointlargeprint.com